CW01426146

TEN LITTLE GIRLS

A REBEKKA FRANCK MYSTERY

WILLOW ROSE

BOOKS BY THE AUTHOR

HARRY HUNTER MYSTERY SERIES

- ALL THE GOOD GIRLS
- RUN GIRL RUN
- NO OTHER WAY
- NEVER WALK ALONE

MARY MILLS MYSTERY SERIES

- WHAT HURTS THE MOST
- YOU CAN RUN
- YOU CAN'T HIDE
- CAREFUL LITTLE EYES

EVA RAE THOMAS MYSTERY SERIES

- DON'T LIE TO ME
- WHAT YOU DID
- NEVER EVER
- SAY YOU LOVE ME
- LET ME GO
- IT'S NOT OVER
- TO DIE FOR

EMMA FROST SERIES

- ITSY BITSY SPIDER
- MISS DOLLY HAD A DOLLY
- RUN, RUN AS FAST AS YOU CAN
- CROSS YOUR HEART AND HOPE TO DIE
- PEEK-A-BOO I SEE YOU
- TWEEDLEDUM AND TWEEDLEDEE

- Easy as One, Two, Three
- There's No Place like Home
- Slenderman
- Where the Wild Roses Grow
- Waltzing Mathilda
- Drip Drop Dead
- Black Frost

JACK RYDER SERIES

- Hit the Road Jack
- Slip out the Back Jack
- The House that Jack Built
- Black Jack
- Girl Next Door
- Her Final Word
- Don't Tell

REBEKKA FRANCK SERIES

- One, Two…He is Coming for You
- Three, Four…Better Lock Your Door
- Five, Six…Grab your Crucifix
- Seven, Eight…Gonna Stay up Late
- Nine, Ten…Never Sleep Again
- Eleven, Twelve…Dig and Delve
- Thirteen, Fourteen…Little Boy Unseen
- Better Not Cry
- Ten Little Girls
- It Ends Here

MYSTERY/THRILLER/HORROR NOVELS

- In One Fell Swoop

- UMBRELLA MAN
- BLACKBIRD FLY
- TO HELL IN A HANDBASKET
- EDWINA

HORROR SHORT-STORIES

- MOMMY DEAREST
- THE BIRD
- BETTER WATCH OUT
- EENIE, MEENIE
- ROCK-A-BYE BABY
- NIBBLE, NIBBLE, CRUNCH
- HUMPTY DUMPTY
- CHAIN LETTER

PARANORMAL SUSPENSE/ROMANCE NOVELS

- IN COLD BLOOD
- THE SURGE
- GIRL DIVIDED

THE VAMPIRES OF SHADOW HILLS SERIES

- FLESH AND BLOOD
- BLOOD AND FIRE
- FIRE AND BEAUTY
- BEAUTY AND BEASTS
- BEASTS AND MAGIC
- MAGIC AND WITCHCRAFT
- WITCHCRAFT AND WAR
- WAR AND ORDER

- Order and Chaos
- Chaos and Courage

THE AFTERLIFE SERIES

- Beyond
- Serenity
- Endurance
- Courageous

THE WOLFBOY CHRONICLES

- A Gypsy Song
- I am WOLF

DAUGHTERS OF THE JAGUAR

- Savage
- Broken

CHAPTER ONE

May 2018

"*One little, two little, three little children...*"

The man watching the children play at the school's playground was drumming his fingers on his thighs while singing the song in a low voice.

"*Four little, five little, six little children...*"

It was a gorgeous day out. The sun was shining above him and making him sweat. It was very hot, but that wasn't unusual for this time of year in Florida. The man liked the heat. He always had. He enjoyed the feeling of sweat prickling on his skin. He enjoyed his shirt being soaked and the feeling of almost unbearably moist air inside his lungs.

It made him feel at home.

The children on the playground were laughing. A group of five kids was playing hide and go seek, and the man smiled widely. He had been watching them for months now from between the trees, observing their every move, until he knew everything there was to know about them, everything he needed to know, and his absolute favorite part was when they played that.

From where he was standing, he could see where everyone was hiding. He giggled when the girl who was *it* came close to a boy hiding beneath the slides, but she couldn't see him, so she turned and walked away. She found another boy hiding behind a bush not far from where the man was standing. The man giggled as the girl yelled *Found You,* and the boy started to run. The girl set off after him, but unfortunately, she tripped. The boy didn't notice and kept running. Meanwhile, the girl had scraped her knee and started to cry, sitting on the ground holding her leg. The teacher didn't see it. She was standing in the shade, talking to her colleague from the other class.

The girl was crying helplessly now as she spotted blood coming from her scrape. Still, the teacher saw nothing. It annoyed the man, and he had to bite down hard on his lip, so he wouldn't yell and reveal himself. He clenched his fists so hard his nails dug into the palms of his hands and left marks.

Finally, the boy she had been chasing noticed what had happened to her. He walked up to the teacher and told her about the girl who was crying. The teacher walked to the girl and looked at her scrape, then helped her get up. She said something to the other teacher, then got ahold of another student who helped the girl who was hurt get to the clinic.

The man relaxed again.

The kids continued playing till recess was over and the teacher told them to line up. A few minutes later, they all walked in a long line back to class before the next class arrived and filled the playground with joy as they played. It was the same every day, and the man couldn't stop watching it. It was too bad he soon had to. Soon, there would be no more children on the playground. There would be no more laughter. Yet there would still be playing.

An entirely new game of hide and go seek was about to begin.

CHAPTER TWO

September 1990

J
ane and Bob were young when they got married. They knew
they were, but it didn't matter, they thought. They loved each
other and had since they met in high school. For Jane, Bob was
her first and only boyfriend, and she knew she wanted to spend the
rest of her life with him. There was no doubt in her mind; he was
the one for her.

So, at the age of only nineteen, they got *hitched*, as their friends
called it. They *tied the knot, took the plunge, bought the cow.*

It wasn't a big wedding, but it was just the way they wanted it to
be. A small ceremony on the beach, with their toes dug deep in the
white Florida sand and the wind so strong in Jane's hair that she had
to hold onto her veil, so it wouldn't fly away.

For their honeymoon, they went to Disney World and stayed two
nights at the Disney Resort. It was a wedding present from Bob's
mother, who couldn't afford much but had saved up to be able to
give it to them.

Jane had never been happier in her life. Even though she grew
up in Central Florida, she had never been to Disney World. Since
her mom was a single mother to her and her brother, she could

never afford to take her there or anywhere else that cost money, despite working two jobs.

Once the honeymoon was over, they moved to Cocoa Beach. Bob had gotten a job at a roofing company, and the two of them moved into a one-bedroom condo only steps from the beach. Meanwhile, Jane got a job at Ron Jon's, the world's largest surf shop, in the swimsuit department.

Everything was coming together for the young couple quickly. Bob adored her and worshipped the ground that Jane walked on. He surprised her by coming to her work and taking her out for lunch; he showered her with presents, flowers, and sometimes even chocolate. He would have the flowers sent to her job to brighten up her day. She loved that he did that, even though her co-worker one day said she thought he only did it to, "Piss on his territory and make sure everyone knew she was taken."

Jane understood that her co-worker obviously was just jealous because she and Bob had such a great marriage. Why else would she say such a silly thing?

"Bob is just kind and very generous," Jane replied and held the flowers in her hands.

"Tell me, when is the last time you did anything with anyone else but him?" the co-worker then asked.

"What do you mean?" Jane asked.

"When was the last time you went out with friends?"

"I…I don't really have many friends."

The co-worker gave her a look that made Jane feel very uncomfortable. She had a lump in her throat and hurried into the back, still holding the flowers. She found a vase for them and smelled them, annoyed at her co-worker for saying such a stupid thing and ruining the gift for her. It was true what they said: jealousy really was such an ugly green monster. Jane then decided to be careful not to let people like her co-worker get between her and her happiness. She couldn't let this get to her the way it had.

Yet later in the day, when another co-worker, Tim, asked if she would go out for lunch with him and a couple of others, Jane said yes, even though she usually would have said no.

CHAPTER THREE

May 2018

For eight-year-old Alicia Porter, going to school had stopped being fun the day that her best friend Alondra had ditched her for Tonya Reynolds. Up until then, Alondra and Alicia had been inseparable. Ever since Kindergarten. They would always hang together at recess and play their wolf-game, where they pretended to be half-wolves in a pack. They would sit next to one another on the bus on the way home and even often play after school since they lived so close together.

But two weeks ago, Tonya had stolen Alondra from Alicia since her best friend, Samantha, had ditched her for Mercedes, the new girl in their class. Alicia used to love school, but since that happened, she always felt so alone on the playground and even in the classroom since she no longer had a best friend to hang out with.

Today was no different. At lunch, she had walked up to Alondra and asked if she could sit with her, but Alondra had just looked at her, then turned around and talked to Tonya instead. Alicia had sat down anyway, but all during lunch break, Alondra had kept her back turned to her, so she couldn't even see her face. Then she and Tonya took a selfie with Alondra's new phone. Alondra was the first one in their class to get one. Alicia had tried to be a part of it, poking her head up between them, but they had just turned away and taken the picture without her.

That almost made Alicia cry, but she held it back. She didn't want her classmates to see her sad, so she put on a brave face and pretended like she didn't care. But the fact was, she was all alone. Everyone else had someone…a best friend they could hang out with. For a few seconds, she thought about telling the teachers that Alondra had her phone out during school hours, but Alicia knew nothing good would come from it. They would only end up hating her and avoiding her even more.

Alicia bit her lip, hard, in order not to cry and that was how she made it through the rest of the day. In the afternoon, when the bell rang, and they were told to go to the bus, Alicia grabbed her backpack and hurried out to the line as fast as she was allowed to—without running in the hallway and getting herself in trouble. She stood in the line outside by the bus, waiting for it to open, when Alondra and Tonya came up behind her, laughing about something.

Alicia closed her eyes and wished herself far away. If only she could change schools or even get homeschooled. Anything was better than having to look at those two every day. Anything was better than being alone all the time.

Can't wait for summer break.

Alicia had tried to talk to her mother about her problems, but she didn't seem to understand it much and would always say something lame like: "This too shall pass." Or, "I went through the same when I was your age. You'll find someone else, another best friend. A year from now, what will it matter?"

To Alicia, it mattered a great deal; in fact, so much that she tried hard to come up with an excuse every morning not to have to go to school. But her mother never believed her when she said she was sick. Not as long as she didn't have a fever.

Can't I just get a fever? Can't I just get sick for real? Please, God? Make me sick for a very long time.

When Alicia felt a tap on her shoulder, and she was told she was going on a different bus today, she felt such relief. At least she wouldn't have to listen to them as they giggled and had a great time. At least she could relax on the way home.

Little did she know, she wasn't going home.

CHAPTER FOUR

May 2018

"The bus is late. Again."

Sue Porter, who was standing next to me, sighed and looked at her watch.

"Can you believe it? I don't have time for this," she said addressed to the third mother, Nancy, standing with us on the sidewalk.

I had William with me, and he was getting tired of standing and wanted me to pick him up, so I did. It was really hot out, and a thunderstorm was approaching in the distance. It was the same every afternoon when waiting for Julie and Tobias to come home from school.

We had been in Florida for five months now, and I was beginning to really enjoy it. I loved the heat, even though it was a getting to be a little much as summer approached. I still preferred it to the cold at home. Things were just easier when it was warm. The kids needed fewer clothes, and we spent many hours outside, a lot more than back home. The kids usually jumped in the pool right after school and stayed there for hours. They were hardly on their computers or iPads anymore, not until late in the evening or some days not at all. We had rented a house on the beach in Cocoa Beach for an entire year. It was expensive but completely worth it. I loved everything about it. Especially the pool and the beach right in the backyard. It doesn't get much better than that.

I was trying hard to get my freelance career up and running and, so far, I had gotten lots of jobs. Mostly from Danish newspapers who wanted me to write stories about Disney World and travel tips for Danes wanting to go abroad for the summer. It was easy to write these articles, and they required very little work on my part. A magazine had even given me a column where I was to write about what it was like to rip an entire year out of the calendar and live somewhere else. The articles paid well, and it was just enough to keep us afloat since my boyfriend Sune still couldn't work. He was the reason we had come to Florida in the first place. So he finally could get the help he needed. He was making great progress. Working with Dr. Herman at his clinic on Merritt Island had made him capable of getting out of the wheelchair completely, and he was walking now, only needing a walker every now and then, especially on longer strolls. He would be able to walk normally and even run again within the next six months, Dr. Herman had promised us.

After two years bound to a wheelchair because of being shot in the stomach, that was exactly the kind of news that Sune needed. Heck, it was what we all needed. It was just the turn-around we had prayed for. Sune fought hard every day and came home exhausted, but he felt the progress himself and—best of all—he was happy.

The kids went to the local school, Theodore Roosevelt Elementary, and it hadn't taken them long to make friends, even though it had been easier for Julie than for Tobias, who struggled more with the language than his stepsister. Tobias had to take extra English lessons to keep up, while they said Julie didn't need to. It was quite a blow to him, but he was a tough boy, and I was certain he would get through it. And once he did, he would be the best in his English class once we returned to Denmark. If we ever returned. I wasn't sure I wanted to go back. I was really enjoying myself here.

"Now, I have never…this is the latest it has ever been," Sue Porter said with a snort.

She was one of our neighbors, and her daughter Alicia had

been over to play with our children a few times, even though she was a lot younger than Julie. The third mom, Nancy Browning, stayed a little behind us. Her daughter, Alondra, was also on the bus. There was some quarrel between the two of them that I didn't really want to get into, but each of them had entertained me about it on occasion when we were alone. It was between their children but had soon grown to be about the adults as well, apparently. It was the kind of drama I didn't want any part of.

"Don't they know that people have things to do?" Sue asked and looked first at Nancy then at me. I shrugged. I had an article I needed to finish, but I wasn't really in a rush.

"I see it now," I said and pointed down A1A where the yellow bus was approaching. "It's on its way."

"About darn time," Sue Porter said with another snort. "Some of us actually have a life."

CHAPTER FIVE

May 2018

The bus blinked its yellow lights to let everyone know it was about to stop, then slung out its red stop signs on the sides. One car, a black Camaro, slipped past it just as the bus sighed deeply and slowed down. The bus driver honked angrily at the black Camaro, but it was already long gone.

The two moms standing on each side of me, approaching the stopping bus, shook their heads with a *tsk*.

The bus sighed, satisfied, and came to a complete stop. Small heads were on the move inside of it, and the door hissed open. The first kid was a fifth-grade boy that lived across the street from us, whose mom was never around to pick him up. He stumbled out, swinging his heavy backpack onto his shoulders, then rushed across the street. Next came Tobias. I smiled and waved.

William saw him and shrieked with joy.

"Tubby!"

I put him down, so he could run to his older brother.

"Not now, Will," Tobias grumbled. He was almost always in a terrible mood when coming home from school. William didn't seem to take any notice and just hugged his leg. It made Tobias smile. I noticed he was sweating. His bangs were wet.

"There was no AC on the bus," he said and wiped his forehead. "It broke."

Another boy, Alondra's brother, J.T., emerged from the bus and rushed to his mom. He was a Kindergartener and so small I could hardly believe it. He was even smaller than William, who was only four years old. He and William had played together several times and got along pretty well. It was great to have children close by that my kids could play with.

I hugged Tobias, even though he was sweaty. Behind him, the bus hissed again as the doors closed and it was about to take off. The Stop signs were pulled in and my heart sunk.

"Julie?" I asked. "Where's Julie?" Panic erupted instantaneously, and I let go of Tobias, then ran to the bus.

"HEY!"

I reached the door and knocked on it, hard, while yelling for it to stop. It did, and the driver opened the door again.

"Where's my daughter? Where's Julie?" I asked, almost finding it too hard even to get the words across my lips. My heart was pounding so hard in my chest; I could hardly breathe.

Easy, Rebekka. Calm down.

The two other moms came up behind me. Their voices were trembling as badly as mine.

"Where's my daughter?" Sue asked. "Where's Alicia?"

"And Alondra?" Nancy asked.

"Where are our children?" I asked.

The female bus driver shrugged. "I don't know. They didn't get on the bus."

"You mean to say they're still at the school?" I asked, getting more annoyed now. Had Julie missed the bus somehow? Was she goofing around?

The bus driver shrugged again. "I don't know."

"You don't know?" Sue asked. "You don't know? You're responsible for them, for cryin' out loud."

"Listen, lady. I'm responsible for those children that *do* enter my bus, not the ones that don't. Now, maybe the school didn't dismiss them in time or somethin'; I don't know, but I gotta get goin'. I have more kids who need to get home before they melt."

And just like that, she closed the doors once again and took off, leaving us three mothers behind—without our daughters.

CHAPTER SIX

May 2018

"I ...I..."

Sue stared at the bus as it left. "I'm calling the school. Immediately."

I turned around to face Tobias, who was still wiping sweat from his face with his arm.

"What?" he asked.

"Where is your sister?" I said. I insisted on calling Julie his sister because I wanted them to feel like they were siblings, even though Sune and I weren't married. We were still a family.

He shrugged. "I don't know. Guess she never made it on the bus."

"How? How could she have missed the bus?" I asked. "I don't get it?"

He shrugged again. "I don't know. She's in another class, remember? They come out after we do."

"And you didn't notice she wasn't on the bus when it took off?" I asked, sounding a lot more accusatory than I intended.

"Not really. She usually sits all the way up front, and I was with Brandon. I didn't really notice."

I ran a hand through my hair. "I guess we'll have to go pick her up by car then."

I drew in a deep breath and looked at my watch. William was petting Nancy's dog that she always brought when picking up her kids. I looked at Sue, who was busy on the phone. She was getting paler and paler. Then she hung up, an anxious expression on her face. My heart sunk.

"What did they say?" Nancy asked.

Sue shook her head. Her eyes had grown distant and a little feverish. "They don't know where they are either."

I couldn't breathe. "What?"

Sue's eyes grew wild. "They don't know where they are either. They were supposed to be on the bus."

"But they weren't," Nancy said.

"You don't say, Miss Marple," Sue hissed.

"I can't believe this," I said. I looked at Tobias again. "You didn't see her at all?"

"I just expected her to be there," he said. "She usually is."

"Could they have taken another bus?" I asked, focusing on calming myself down. I walked to the road and looked down where the bus usually came from. About ten cars or so passed me, but I couldn't see any bus as far as the eye could see.

"I can't believe this," Sue said. "She could have been kidnapped. What if they were kidnapped?"

"Let's not get ahead of ourselves here," I said, speaking just as much to calm myself down. "There has to be a logical explanation. I'm sure there is. They were probably just put on the wrong bus."

"What if they weren't?" Sue said, getting herself more and more worked up. "What if they were kidnapped?"

"Three children at the same time?" I said. "That sounds very unlikely. Let's keep it to realistic scenarios."

"Rebekka is right," Nancy said. "Let's stay calm for a second here. They're probably just on a different bus and, if we wait a little longer, they'll probably come home or be driven back to the school and then they'll call us."

"Okay," Sue said, taking in a deep breath. "Let's wait a little longer."

CHAPTER SEVEN

September 1990

They went to the port for lunch, and Jane ordered a mahi-mahi sandwich, jerked, the way she preferred it. Jane enjoyed being out with her co-workers and especially enjoyed listening to them tell stories about the manager and about things that had happened before she came to work at Ron Jon's. It felt good to be with other people besides Bob. She realized she had missed it. She only wished he could be there too...to hear all of Tim's jokes and listen to Annabelle giggle. She was going to tell Bob all about it once she got home. The two others, Annabelle and Landon, who worked in accounting, left early since they had a meeting they had to go to, and soon it was just her and Tim left sitting at Captain Ed's Seafood Restaurant at Port Canaveral, finishing up their food. Jane listened politely as Tim told her all about his wife and two boys and how one of them couldn't say *I beg your pardon* properly and explained that it usually came out *I beg your apartment*, and also how the other one usually woke him up early in the morning by crawling on top of him with his wet diaper.

It was all very cute, but Jane soon found it slightly boring. You probably had to have children of your own to understand. Jane and

Bob had talked about children, but Jane wasn't really ready yet. She wanted to wait a few years more, while Bob wanted to start now.

"How about you?" Tim asked slurping his soda. "Any kids?"

She shook her head and finished her sandwich. She was getting ready to go back. Her lunch break was almost over.

Tim was kind enough to pick up the check and, as they were about to get up, Jane suddenly spotted a familiar face approaching their table.

Jane smiled widely at the sight of her husband. "Hi, hon. What are you doing here?"

He had a strange look on his face, a flustered one that Jane didn't immediately recognize.

"I...I wanted to surprise you for lunch, so I went to pick you up, and guess what? You weren't there."

He ran a hand through his hair, laughing awkwardly.

"They told me you were here, and guess what? There you are with...I'm sorry, I didn't catch your name?"

Tim cleared his throat. "Tim Stover. I work in men's underwear."

Bob chuckled nervously. "Of course, you do."

"I'm sorry, babe. I already ate," Jane said. "I'm sorry for ruining your surprise."

"Ruining it! Ruining it? No...it was a surprise alright."

"O-okay. But we have to get back now. My lunch break is over in a few minutes," she said.

Bob gave her a strange look. Then he forced a smile. It came off very awkward.

"Of course. Let me give you a ride back."

Jane nodded, thanked Tim for lunch, then got in the truck. Bob put the key in the ignition and started it up with a deep roar. He was about to back out of the spot when he hesitated, then killed the engine instead.

"Say...who's Tim and how long have you been sleeping with him?"

Jane's eyes grew wide. "Excuse me?"

"Don't give me that."

"What are you talking about? You saw us; we were just having lunch. There were others there earlier, but they had to leave. I only stayed to finish my food and because Tim had promised me a ride back."

"You don't think I know what you two were doing? You think I am *that* stupid?"

Jane felt her cheeks grow red. She really hadn't thought about it at all. There had never been jealousy between them, and she didn't think either of them had it in them.

"No. I don't think you're stupid at all."

"Well, you must since…you're obviously going behind my back."

"What? No, you don't…"

Jane stopped talking and sunk into the seat. She felt awful. Of course, it looked like she was alone with Tim. Heck, it almost looked like they had been on a date with him paying for her food and all. She couldn't believe she had been so stupid and insensitive toward Bob. She would have thought the same thing if she saw Bob out with some woman, wouldn't she? It was all just a stupid misunderstanding.

"I am sorry," she said and grabbed his arm. "I really am. But nothing is going on. It was just a lunch. I can assure you. It was very innocent."

Bob drew in a deep breath. He placed his hand on top of hers and looked into her eyes.

"I believe you," he said. "And I forgive you."

She smiled in relief. "Thank you, hon."

He started the truck back up. "No problem. Just don't talk to him again, okay?"

Bob turned his head to back up. Jane looked at him. Had he just said that? Had she heard him right? No, it couldn't be.

"Excuse me…what?" she asked.

He maneuvered the car out of the parking lot. "You heard me. Just don't talk to that Tim guy ever again, okay?"

"How am I supposed to do that?" Jane asked, completely stupefied. "We work together?"

Bob stopped at a red light. "You'll figure it out; I'm sure. And don't wear those pants again. They're too tight."

Jane's eyes grew wide. She didn't know what to say. She felt so guilty for having been so inconsiderate toward him; she would do anything to make him happy again.

"You don't like my pants?" she asked.

"Oh, I love them, but they kind of send the wrong signal if you know what I mean."

She didn't, but she didn't dare tell him. Instead, she simply nodded.

"O-okay."

"Maybe I should help you pick out your clothes from now on. The ones you wear for work. Just to make sure people like Tim don't get the wrong impression, huh?"

Jane stared at her husband, completely baffled. She felt it was a harsh punishment and that he was kind of going too far, but still, she didn't say anything. She wanted him to forgive her completely and wanted it all to be over.

So, she agreed.

CHAPTER EIGHT
May 2018

Half an hour later, I was racing down Minutemen Causeway. Sue Porter and Nancy Browning were both with me. We had left William and J.T. with Tobias and Sune. We had waited twenty more minutes to see if another bus would come down A1A carrying our children, but none did.

Now, I was about to explode. I too had called the school and asked Miss Elaine at the front desk where my child was, and she had given me the same response she had given Sue earlier.

She didn't know.

"Well, who does know then?" I had asked, enraged.

Miss Elaine's voice had been cracking by this point. "I...I don't know!"

It was a school zone, and I was definitely not allowed to go as fast as I was, but at this point, I didn't care. I needed to get back there and look for my daughter.

I had tried calling her cell—of course I had, endlessly—but it went to her voicemail since it was turned off as usual during school hours. She wasn't even allowed to take it out on the bus.

I parked the car in the parking lot, swinging it around so fast the two other women shrieked. And then my heart dropped...again.

In front of the school, two police cars were parked. I spotted two officers in the middle of a crowd of parents. I didn't have to open the door to know that they were agitated and yelling at each other. I could tell by their strained faces and the wide gesticulation of arms.

"What the heck is going on here?" Sue asked.

I took in a deep breath and turned off the engine. "I guess we should go find out."

The deep sensation of dread and fear was gnawing from the inside as we walked up toward the scene. I could now hear the parents yelling at the officers, while poor Miss Elaine hid behind one of them.

"If you can't tell us where our kids are, then who can?" a dad said. His face was red with agitation.

"Trudy was supposed to be home long ago! She has lacrosse practice," a mom said.

"Aubrey has cheer," another mom said.

"I know. I know, we all want you to find your children," the officer said.

"So, why aren't you helping?" someone yelled from the back.

"Yes, what exactly are you doing?" a mom chimed in, crossing her arms in front of her chest.

The officer cleared his throat. "We've called for help."

"Help? What kind of help?"

"Have you contacted the buses? I tried to call earlier, but they kept sending me to someone else and no one could answer my questions," the dad from earlier said, clenching his fist.

"Let's try and remain…"

"How about you, Miss Elaine?" a mom said. Her voice sounded more concerned than angry "When did you see them last?"

"Now, there's no use for anyone to be asking…" the officer started, standing between Miss Elaine and the crowd. "Miss Elaine here has told us everything she knows. All we know for now is they were all supposed to be on the bus, right?"

"Right," someone mumbled.

"Where's Mrs. Chapman?"

"Yeah, where is she?" someone chimed in. "She's supposed to be the principal, isn't she?"

"We demand to talk to her."

"Yeah. We need answers."

"Mrs. Chapman is at a meeting inland," the officer said. "She left around lunchtime. She's on her way back now. But Miss Elaine here tells us that everything went as normal this afternoon at dismissal. Your children all left the school area this afternoon as planned. They were lined up for the buses as usual but, somehow, they didn't get on. That's what we know so far."

"How the heck is that even possible?" another angry dad asked. "How can a thing like this happen?"

"We leave the kids in your care," a woman said addressed to the small and chubby Miss Elaine, who had started to cry. "We expect you to make sure they come home."

I didn't quite understand why they were being so harsh on Miss Elaine since she was, after all, just the front office clerk; she had nothing to do with getting the kids on the buses at dismissal. But I guess she was the only one there, and we all needed someone, a face, to address our questions to.

"What about the buses?" the dad from earlier repeated. "The kids were their responsibility as soon as they left the school, right? What do they have to say for themselves? Is there a bus out there somewhere that has taken the wrong route or something?"

"We're talking with them right now," the officer said. I could tell he was in over his head. "So far, they're telling us that all the kids that were on the buses this afternoon have been dropped off."

"But they never came home," a dad said.

"We are aware of that," someone else cut in. He stepped forward, and I recognized Detective Jack Ryder. I knew him because he had helped me on a case around Christmas and we'd had him and his family over for dinner a few times since then.

My eyes locked with his. This was no time for catching up or even smiling at one another, though.

"Listen, guys. You've got to know that everyone is doing everything they can to figure this out. But you've got to give them some space to work."

"So, what are you doing about it?" another dad said. "Are we supposed to just stand here and wait? How do I know you're even doing all you can to get my daughter home?"

Jack put a hand on the man's shoulder. "Believe me, John, you know I have kids of my own in this school. I will do everything— and I do mean everything—in my power to get those kids back to you."

I could tell by the look on John's face that he knew Jack would. I just hoped and prayed it was enough.

CHAPTER NINE

May 2018

"Apparently, they were told to go on another bus."

We were all sitting in the commons area inside the school, waiting for news of our kids. Detective Jack Ryder had left for about twenty minutes, and now he had come back. I had started biting my nails while texting Sune, who was still back at the house and wanted to know what was going on. The woman next to me started sobbing. Her hands were shaking while holding her phone. She kept staring at it, checking if there was a signal every few seconds, her fingers frantically tapping the display.

"What do you mean they were told to go on another bus?" a dad said getting up from the bench.

All eyes were on the detective. He ran a hand through his long blond hair. His blue eyes told me he didn't have good news.

"We have spoken to several of the kids who were on the bus and who stood in the line outside while they waited for the bus, the way they usually do. A kid told us some of the kids in line were told to go on another bus today. The girl standing in front of him was one of them, he said."

"Another bus? What other bus? And how is that even possible?"

the same dad asked. "Wasn't there a teacher present? Wasn't anyone supervising them?"

"That's what we're trying to figure out," Jack said. "According to Miss Elaine, it's usually Mrs. Braddock who supervises the buses, but she wasn't here today. She's at her cousin's wedding in Oklahoma. Mr. Meckler filled in for her today. He might have messed up and sent some children on the wrong bus. That's our theory so far."

Jack looked down at his phone as it was ringing. "I have to get this," he said and left.

The dad sighed and looked at the rest of us. "I can't believe this. This is all we get? Mrs. Braddock was gone, and then it all goes to hell in a handbasket?"

"Yeah, what were they doing putting the kids on a different bus anyway?" a mom asked. "Who told them to do it?"

"I bet Mr. Meckler is behind this," another mom said. I knew her as Mary but had never learned her last name. She was the mother of a girl named Haley in Julie's class. "I never trusted him much."

"What are you talking about?" Nancy said. "He's the nicest teacher. Why would he have anything to do with this?"

Mary shrugged. "I don't know. I just never trusted him."

"Because he's a man, is that it? He's the only male teacher we have," Nancy said.

"He's also new. Why do you choose to become a teacher when you're a male anyway?" Mary asked. "Studies have shown that forty-nine percent of kids that are molested are abused by their teachers."

"Where did you get that number?" John asked. "I, for one, think it's great to have a male teacher at the school. The kids need a good male role model as well as a female. I have a son who was in Mr. Meckler's class, and he loved him."

"All the kids love him," Nancy said.

"But still," Mary argued. "There was that story of Adrian, remember? When he was in Mr. Meckler's fifth-grade class, he said Mr. Meckler had grop…"

"That case was dropped," John said, raising his voice. "Adrian lied. He admitted it himself. There is nothing to it."

"Maybe," Mary snorted. "But right now, our kids are missing, and I'm putting my money on Mr. Meckler. He did something to them."

"Please, stop pointing fingers till we know more about what really happened," a mom interrupted them. "Please, just stop it. You're making the rest of us even more nervous. We don't even know if anything bad has happened. Maybe they're just on this other bus somewhere and…well, maybe something happened to the driver of the bus or something. He could have had a stroke, and maybe he parked safely on the side of the road because he wasn't feeling well. Something like that. We still don't know that anything bad has happened, so please stop talking like it has."

"Wouldn't the police have found the bus by now?" Sue asked. "If it was parked in some rest area or on the side of the road?"

"Who knows…?" John said. "It could be a possibility."

"Wouldn't our kids have turned on their phones by now and called us?" Mary said.

That made all the parents stop talking and look down at the phones in their hands.

I looked at Jack Ryder, who was walking up and down the hallway while on his phone. My eyes met his in a quick glance, and I got the distinct feeling there was something he wasn't telling us.

CHAPTER TEN

May 2018

Alicia was sitting next to Julie on the bus. Behind her sat Alondra and Tonya, giggling and having all the fun in the world. When she was told to go on another bus, Alicia had been certain she wouldn't have to deal with them, but they too had come onboard the new bus, much to Alicia's regret.

Alicia didn't know Julie very well, and she was a little older than her, so they didn't talk much. She knew her because they were neighbors and Alicia had hung out at her house a few times since they came here from Denmark. Alicia liked Julie but was a little scared of talking to her since she was a sixth grader and Alicia had just started third grade.

They had been driving forever, and Alicia was beginning to get hot. There was no AC on the bus and no open windows. Alicia looked out the window and didn't recognize anything. It wasn't their usual way home. And why was it taking such a long time?

One of the girls in the front had told the bus driver earlier that this wasn't the way they usually went, but the driver had simply told her that it was a new route and not to worry about it.

"How long do you think it's gonna take before we're home?" Alicia asked Julie.

Julie shrugged. She looked at her watch. "We're usually home by now."

"I don't recognize anything outside," Alicia said and put her nose to the window to cool it down a little, but even the window felt warm, with the sun burning it from the outside. She turned to look at Julie. "Do you think we're lost?"

Julie grimaced. "I don't know. Maybe."

The bus continued through the landscape that got more and more foreign to Alicia. It kind of reminded her of where her Uncle Ryan lived in the middle of Florida. He had taken her hog hunting once when she came to visit, and she had seen a huge gator in the swamps, eating a poor deer, crunching its bones loudly. The deer had still been alive and watching her with its big brown eyes while the gator slowly devoured it. After that, she told her uncle she never wanted to go into the swamps again.

Ever.

"I think at least we're going in the wrong..." Alicia said when the bus suddenly slowed down and came to a halt.

All the girls looked up from their seats.

"Where are we?" Alondra asked behind Alicia.

"This is not Cocoa Beach," a girl from fifth grade named Emmy said.

They looked out the windshield, but there was nothing there. No houses, no buildings, no town. Just swamps. Alicia shuddered thinking about the deer in the gator's mouth.

"This is definitely not Cocoa Beach," Alicia said in a low voice. "We are totally lost."

The bus driver got up from his seat and opened the front door. In front of them on the road, two vans were parked. Two men wearing pantyhose over their heads stepped inside the bus. Alicia felt herself grab Julie's hand when she spotted the guns in their hands.

CHAPTER ELEVEN

February 1991

"**D**on't put Sweet-and-Low in your coffee. That stuff is poison for you."

Jane paused midair with the bag between her fingers. Then she put it down. Bob was right; that stuff was dangerous. She just really liked her coffee sweetened, and since Bob had told her to stop using real sugar if she wanted to lose weight, the sweetener was all she had left. But he was right. She really shouldn't put it in. If the coffee wasn't sweet, then chances were, she would drink less of it too, so maybe that was even healthier.

She sipped the bitter coffee and swallowed. Bob had taken her out for brunch this Sunday as he often did, generous and thoughtful as he was. Jane felt his hand touch her thigh under the table and she giggled. He leaned over and kissed her, gentle and caring as ever.

Things had been really good between them the past several months. He was so considerate it was hard to believe. Even their sex was good. And he made sure she had everything in the world she could ever wish for. Flowers at least once a week, surprise lunches, even jewelry when it wasn't her birthday or an anniversary. He liked to surprise her, he said. She always felt so embarrassed since she didn't get him anything. But he didn't want anything other than just to see her happy, he usually said.

"Is that a new nail polish?" he asked, looking at her hand in his.

"Yes, I put it on this morning. You like it?"

He made a face.

"You don't?" she asked, surprised.

"It's all right."

"You're lying. I can tell you don't like it, do you?" she asked a little disappointed. She had hoped he would.

"It makes you look like a bimbo," he said and drank from his glass of orange juice.

"Excuse me?"

"You know," he said with a shrug after swallowing. "Cheap."

"Really? I didn't even think about that," she said and hid her nails in her lap, so no one could see them.

"Good thing you have me to think for you, huh?" he said with a chuckle.

She nodded, biting her lip, thinking about a call she had received the night before from her best friend, Annabelle. She had told her she missed seeing Jane and that she wanted to go out for lunch soon or something.

"Even just a cup of coffee would do," she said.

"I don't really have time," Jane had told her. "You know how life gets sometimes. Busy, busy, busy!"

That was when Annabelle had gone quiet on the other end. "He doesn't like me, does he?"

"What? No, no, he doesn't know you, Annabelle."

"I haven't seen you in six months; what the heck is going on? Is he telling you who to see and who not to see?"

"No. Of course not."

"Then why do you keep blowing me off?" Annabelle asked.

Jane hadn't known what to say. She loved Annabelle, she really did, but she was right; Bob couldn't stand her. He thought she was bad news for Jane because she wasn't married.

"She doesn't understand that you're a married woman now," he would say. "You have obligations; she doesn't. You're different now, in another league than her. She wants to go out and find men; you don't."

He was right, Jane thought to herself as she watched him shovel scrambled eggs into his mouth. She really shouldn't be hanging out with someone like Annabelle. Not that she didn't want to, she just didn't want to go through all the trouble of Bob nagging at her for being with her. She didn't like that he couldn't stand her, but he was her husband now, and she had to put their marriage before anything else. She was a married woman, and that meant her lifestyle had to change.

CHAPTER TWELVE

May 2018

W e were sent home. After two hours of waiting at the school for news about our children, the police told us to go home and stay by the phone. They had all our numbers and would make sure to call us as soon as they knew more.

We all did as we were told, reluctantly. I, for one, believed it was best for all of us. The atmosphere in the commons room had become quite nasty. There had been a lot of arguing and pointing of fingers, and Mary had insisted that Mr. Meckler had kidnapped all ten girls. It became so bad that John almost punched her at one point.

At the house, Sune was waiting with Tobias and William. He was holding onto his walker but let go of it when he saw me come in.

"Rebekka!"

We hugged, and William joined in by hugging my leg.

"So, there's no news at all?" he asked when we had let go of one another. I spotted Tobias sitting in the kitchen. His eyes were avoiding mine.

"All they know is that ten girls have gone missing. All of them were told to go on another bus, but they don't know who told them that yet, nor do they know where the bus went after it left the school grounds. It's like it vanished. They've put out a search for it all over the county, but we don't know much about what it looks like. We just know what the kids told the police...that it was smaller than the normal buses and that it had dark tinted windows."

Tobias pretended to be playing on his iPad, but I could tell he was listening in on our conversation. I walked to him and sat down.

"Tobias? Look at me."

He lifted his head hesitantly.

"It's not your fault, okay?"

He swallowed. "But...but...I was there."

"So were a lot of other kids; they didn't do anything wrong either. Still not your fault. Do you hear me?"

"I hear you, but it's not true. Julie is my sister. She's my best friend. I should have stopped it. I should have seen where she went."

Tobias got up and rushed to the bathroom, where he closed the door. I walked to the door and could hear him crying on the other side of it.

"Tobias, please. Come on out," his dad yelled. "We need to stand together as a family in this."

"But you hate me! I let this happen!"

"No," I said. "No one hates you. No one believes you could have done anything."

The door opened, and Tobias peeked out. "But..."

I grabbed him and pulled him into a hug. "It's okay. We'll get her home. It's probably just all a big misunderstanding. She'll be home soon."

"You...you think so?"

"Of course."

"Yay," William yelled from the other end of the living room. "Juju home soon!"

My eyes met Sune's, and he could tell I was lying. I didn't believe it one bit. Inside of me, everything was screaming loudly in panic. But I couldn't let the kids sense that. I simply couldn't. Especially not Tobias, not my sensitive stepson. It would break him.

"I knew something was wrong when Mr. Meckler asked Haley to come with him," he said and let go of me.

"What did you say?"

"Haley," he said.

"No, the other part."

"Mr. Meckler?"

"Yes, what did he do?"

"He told Haley to come with him. She was in front of me in the line when he tapped on her shoulder."

CHAPTER THIRTEEN

May 2018

"It was Mr. Meckler, wasn't it?"

I was so angry I was about to explode. I had seen it in Jack's eyes when he was on the phone at the school. He knew Mary was right. I held the phone close to my ear while walking into the back of the house where William wouldn't make too much noise.

"Rebekka…you know I can't answer that," Jack said.

"He's the one who told them to go on another bus, am I right?" I asked, not caring what he was allowed to tell me and what he wasn't. Jack and I had been involved in a case before, and I felt like we could be honest with one another.

He let out a heartfelt sigh. "I can't tell you about it because, if I do, then other parents might hear it and then the speculations will run wild, and I am not about to start a witch-hunt here, Rebekka. I am trying to get your kids home alive…dang it."

"Tobias told me that he heard Mr. Meckler tell Haley Robinson to get out of the line," I said. "In case you wonder how I know."

"Yeah, well. That's the second kid telling me about Mr. Meckler. I guess it'll be out soon anyway. I was just trying to buy us some time. We have him in for questioning."

"And what does he say?"

"He was in charge of supervising the kids today because Mrs. Braddock was out of town, so he did what he was told. It is true that he tapped Haley on the shoulder and pulled her out of the line, but he says it was because she had forgotten her lunch pack in the hallway. He told her to go get it."

"And then what? What about the other girls?" I asked, trying to keep my voice calm.

"I…I don't know. So far, we only have a couple of witnesses telling us about him talking to Haley, not any other kids. We still haven't talked to all the kids, you know. These things take time."

"So, he didn't tell the girls to go on another bus?" I said and wrinkled my nose.

"Not to my knowledge, no."

My shoulders slumped. "So, he doesn't know what happened to them?"

"He says he doesn't."

"But…he was in charge of supervising them?"

"He had no idea which kid usually went on what bus. He just oversaw them getting in line and onto the buses. But again, that's all according to his own statement," Jack said, sounding tired.

"But he must have seen who told them to go on that other bus, right?" I asked. "Or at least who was driving that other bus?"

"He says he didn't see any unusual activity, no strangers. It was just him and the school nurse."

"The nurse was there? Why?" I asked.

"She helps out with the dismissal procedures."

"Okay. Have you talked to her?" I asked.

I had met Mrs. Baker when Julie was hit by a basketball in the head at PE one day and had to come home with a mild concussion. She was a sweet old lady who had been with the school for decades and knew each and every child.

"Not yet," he said. "We haven't been able to reach her. She's not the type who picks up her cell phone while driving. But it's still early in the afternoon. I've sent a patrol car out to her home but haven't heard from them yet. Now, if you'll get off the phone, then maybe I could call her again."

"Of course," I said.

"We're also having all their phones traced, and I'm waiting for an answer from that. I'm hoping that at least one of the girls left her phone on silent instead of shutting it off completely. I don't know why it takes so long, but apparently, it does."

I nodded, feeling a lump in my throat. "Keep me updated."

"Of course, Rebekka. And I meant what I said. I will do everything I can."

I pressed away a tear. "I know you will, Jack. I know you will."

Then we hung up.

CHAPTER FOURTEEN

May 2018

J ulie held Alicia's hand tightly in hers as the gunmen yelled at them to hand over their phones and put them in the basket that one of the men walked through the bus carrying. No one dared to defy them. Julie looked at her phone in her other hand. It had been shut off when leaving the school, but she had turned it on when she realized the trip was taking longer than usual and when she no longer recognized anything outside the windows. While the gunmen yelled at a girl in front for not wanting to give them her phone, Julie quickly opened messenger and sent her mother a text. The gunman approached her, holding out the basket, his eyes staring at her from behind the pantyhose. The hose made his face distorted and creepy.

"Come on," he said and waved the gun. "I don't have all day."

The man smiled behind the pantyhose, revealing a couple of missing teeth.

"Now!"

Julie reached over and put the phone inside the basket just when the display lit up to let her know that the text was sent. Julie gasped, worried that the man would see it, but the other gunman spoke to him, and he turned his head right at the moment when the phone lit up.

By the time he turned his head back, the phone had gone dark again. Julie held her breath and realized she had been squeezing Alicia's hand hard. As the man turned back, she looked at the young girl next to her. She then tried to let go of her hand, but Alicia wouldn't let her. She put her hand back inside of hers as the bus driver started to yell from the front of the bus.

"Time to get out. Leave your seats, leave your backpacks, and get out."

Alicia and Julie exchanged a quick glance. Julie then looked out the window. "Here?" she mumbled. "What's here?"

They did as they were told and walked out in a line onto the road. Some of the girls were whimpering; others had started to cry. Julie tried hard to remain calm.

"Now, get in," one of the gunmen said and pointed at the two vans parked in front of them. The girls looked at one another with confused eyes.

"I...wanna go home," a little girl cried.

"Shut up," the gunman said and pointed the gun at her.

"I want my mommy," the girl continued, now completely out of it. The gunman was obviously frustrated by her and was about to hit her, when Julie let go of Alicia's hand, ran to the girl, and grabbed her. Julie pulled her back in the line. The girl was still crying helplessly, but Julie held her close to make sure she stayed in the line. She felt the girl shaking. She shushed her when she cried loudly.

"GET IN!" the gunman repeated.

Holding the little girl close, Julie helped her get into the van, then jumped in herself, Alicia right behind them. As soon as all the girls were in, one gunman pulled the sliding door closed and now they were sitting in complete darkness. Julie felt Alicia squeeze her hand hard as the engine roared and the van began to move.

CHAPTER FIFTEEN

April 1991

J ane had been in the bathroom for way too long. She knew Bob
would soon begin to ask questions, yet she couldn't get herself
to go out to him. In her hand, she was holding the pregnancy
test, and she kept staring at it like she expected the result to change
if only she looked at it long enough.

There was a knock.

"Are you okay?"

"I…I'm coming out in a bit."

"Okay. Just checkin'."

Jane looked at her face in the mirror. She had no idea how to
react to this news. A baby? A real live baby was growing inside
of her?

She was thrilled. Of course, she was, but also terrified at the
thought. Was she too young? Had she lived enough, or would she
regret having a child when she was only twenty years old? She
wasn't even old enough to drink alcohol yet. Would she be missing
out on her entire youth? Was it too soon?

Another knock. "Baby, you're scaring me here. Are you sure
you're okay?"

Jane swallowed, then looked down at the stick. Yes, she was okay.

Probably. Everything was going to be okay, wasn't it? Maybe this was exactly what their marriage needed?

Terrified, she put her hand on the handle and opened the door. Bob waited outside.

"What's going on?" he asked, throwing out his arms.

She showed him the stick in her shaking hand.

"What's this?"

He grabbed it and looked at it, then turned it in the light. Finally, he lifted his eyes and met hers.

"I-is th-this what I think it is?"

Jane bit her lip, then nodded.

"Yes."

Bob's eyes grew wide. His mouth was gaping. "A-re y-y-ou, I mean are we…does this mean I'm…?"

She nodded again, holding her breath. Bob let out a gasp, then tumbled backward.

Oh, dear Lord, he's not happy?

Barely had Jane finished the thought and wondered if he too thought it was too early when Bob let out a loud shriek of joy. He grabbed her and lifted her in the air.

"I'm gonna be a daddy!!!"

Jane laughed as he spun her around, holding her around the waist.

"I'm gonna be a daddy!" he repeated. "Ha-ha!"

He put her down, held her face between his hands, and rained kisses down on her. "I can't believe it," he said between kisses. "I am the luckiest man alive. I'm gonna be a real daddy. You have no idea how happy that makes me. You did this. You made me this happy!"

Jane nodded and kissed him back, tears rolling across her cheeks. "I'm happy too."

Bob threw out his arms. "This demands a celebration!"

He grabbed her hand and pulled her into the kitchen. He helped her sit down, then grabbed the phone and called The Pier House Restaurant and reserved a table for the same night. Jane rubbed her stomach, happy yet nervous. Bob hung up, then clasped his hands.

"What can I get you? Something to drink? Water? No, don't get up. I'm gonna spoil you from now on. I'm gonna spoil you rotten. You need a foot massage? Here, let me give you one."

Jane leaned back in the chair with a chuckle while Bob grabbed her feet and started to rub them. Jane closed her eyes and enjoyed it. She loved foot massages more than anything.

"I can't believe I'm gonna be a daddy," he said while rubbing her toes. "And best of all is that now you can quit that silly job."

Jane opened her eyes. "What?"

"Yeah. There's no need for you to work anymore. You're gonna be a mama. And you will be the best one."

"But...But I don't want to quit my job," she said and pulled her foot out of his hands.

"Excuse me?" he said.

"I love my job. I never meant to quit it just because we have children."

"But how are you going to be a mom?" he asked. "I don't understand?"

She shrugged. "Lots of women do it."

He got up from his chair with an angry motion, causing the chair to skid across the floor.

"You mean to tell me you want to be like *them*?"

"What are you talking about? Lots of women do both?"

Jane was so surprised by his reaction. It wasn't something they had ever discussed since she assumed that they agreed on it. She loved her work and her co-workers, plus it meant she had a little extra for herself every month. She liked having a little money to spend. With her not working, money would be tight.

Bob grabbed a plate from the counter and threw it across the kitchen. It smashed against the wall and shattered onto the floor.

"And they are terrible mothers. Do you want to be like them, huh? Do you want to be a TERRIBLE mother too?"

Jane stared at the shattered pieces of the plate, wondering what to do. This was important to her. She wasn't going to let go of her job like that. How could she? It was all she had. It was what kept her sane.

"I can do both, Bob. Listen to me. My mom worked. Your mother worked. It's possible."

That threw Bob into a regular fit. He grabbed the chair he had been sitting on and threw it through the air. It hit the cabinets and made a dent in the wood. Jane shrieked as it flew above her head.

Bob stood above her, pointing his finger at her, his cheeks burning in anger, his eyes on fire.

"No woman of mine will be working. You hear me?" he snorted.

"Okay. Okay," Jane said, holding her hands up to protect herself. He had never hit her, but for the first time, she feared that he would.

"If it means so much to you, I'll quit. Just please stop yelling, please."

CHAPTER SIXTEEN

May 2018

The wait was unbearable. I couldn't sit still; I couldn't stand walking around; I couldn't bear looking at the phone; and I couldn't not look at it. I was constantly pacing around the kitchen, looking at the phone, then putting it down, only to return a few seconds later to look at it.

I just wanted this to be over. I just wanted my Julie back.

William brought me his favorite stuffed animal, an orca that we bought for him at SeaWorld. He handed it to me for comfort, so now I was walking around nervously with a dog-sized stuffed orca under my arm.

The worst part was not being able to do anything. My Julie was out there somewhere, and I didn't know where or who was with her. Was she safe? Was she hungry? Julie was always starving at this time of day after coming home from school.

That was when my phone made a sound. I rushed to the counter and picked it up, then stopped breathing.

"What is it?" Sune asked, approaching me.

"I…It's from Julie…a text…"

I pressed a button and immediately tried to call her back, but only got her voicemail again. I groaned, annoyed.

"You got a text from her? From Julie? Well, what does it say?" he asked.

"I…it's just…it doesn't really say anything. It's just a…" I looked up and met Sune's eyes. "She wrote her own name."

I swallowed and sat down heavily in the chair.

"So, it just says *Julie*?"

I nodded and bit my lip. A tear escaped my eye, and I wiped it away.

"But that means she's fine, right?" Sune asked. "Why are you crying?"

I looked up at him and wiped away another tear. "A few months ago, I had a talk with Julie about bullying and peer pressure. Realizing she would soon be going into middle school, I knew that some of the kids might start smoking and drinking at some point within the next few years. So, we decided that she should have a code word. A word she could write to me, so I would know that she was in trouble and to come get her. A word that if her friends grabbed her phone, they wouldn't know she was asking for me to come for her and wouldn't bully her for it. You know, so they wouldn't come after her saying she was calling for her mama, that she was *running home to mommy*, stuff like that."

"And that word was her own name?"

"Yes. It was something I read in an article somewhere and thought it was clever. This tells me she is in trouble somehow."

"And exactly how were you supposed to find her then, according to your clever plan?" Sune asked.

I lifted my eyes again. Suddenly, a small hope was springing into them. "The app," I said and grabbed my phone from the counter. "You know the one you always say is only for paranoid and overly controlling helicopter moms?"

"The map-one?"

"Yes. It shows me where she is at all times if her phone is turned on. And if she managed to send me this text, then her phone must have been turned on. She must have turned it on even though she usually keeps it shut off on the bus."

I opened the app, tapping hard and frantically on the glass of my phone.

"Well?" Sune said as I zoomed out on the map. Julie's picture showed up, and her whereabouts were pinned on the map.

"Bingo."

CHAPTER SEVENTEEN

May 2018

I called up detective Ryder and told him, but refused to tell him exactly where the app had told me Julie was until he promised to bring me along. There was no way I was going to stay home while knowing where my daughter was. A few minutes later, he drove up in our driveway, and I got into the car.

"You're a very stubborn woman, do you know that?" he asked.

"I've heard that before," I said.

"Okay. So where are we going?"

I opened the app and showed him.

He looked surprised. "That far inland, huh?"

"Apparently so," I said while Jack got the car back onto the road and rushed off. He put the sirens on to clear the roads. Behind us followed three other police cars.

"Once we get there, I want you to stay in the car, you hear me?" he said as we passed a couple of cars that drove onto the side of the road to let us by. "I can't worry about you too. It's the children before anything."

"Naturally," I said. "Let's just find them, okay?"

"I couldn't agree more," he said took a turn so sharp I banged my head against the window.

"Ouch."

"You're the one who wanted to tag along," he said.

I rubbed the side of my head but didn't argue with him. I could tell he was annoyed by me.

"I could have you arrested, you know. For withholding evidence in an ongoing investigation," he continued.

"Then, why didn't you?" I asked.

"Not enough time. Frankly, right now, I just want the girls back."

"Then we can at least agree on something," I said.

He made an annoyed sound as we came across the bridges and hit the mainland. According to the map, Julie was close to St. John's River and Lake Poinsett. We had been there once to go on an airboat ride back in February where we had seen two grown gators and several babies. It was a very remote area with lots of swamps surrounding it. I kept thinking of a logical explanation to why the girls would end up out there, but the most plausible one I could come up with was that the bus driver had somehow lost his mind, maybe gone senile or something and thought they were going on a field trip.

"It's not moving," I said. "Her position on the map. They're standing still. Maybe they parked the bus and are waiting to be found?"

Or maybe the phone has been turned off. You know the location on the map remains in the same place if the phone is turned off.

"One can hope," Jack said and sped up. I had never gone so fast in any car before. Luckily, Jack was a good driver.

As we continued, the residential areas disappeared, and soon there was nothing but swampy marshland on either side of the road. Cows and horses were grassing in the fields surrounded by water, and I wondered how they kept the gators from eating them.

We drove for what felt like forever, going straight forward through swampy and rural areas until we finally came closer to the place where the map told me Julie was. My heart pounded in my chest as we approached the spot, then passed it.

CHAPTER EIGHTEEN

May 2018

"Stop. Stop the car!" I yelled at Jack. I could hardly breathe. This couldn't be true!

"STOP!"

He looked at me, then hit the brakes. The car came to a sudden halt, then skidded sideways. The cars behind us stopped just as abruptly and ended up on the side of the road.

"What? Why?"

"We passed it," I said. "It was back there. Look." I showed him the map. He looked confused.

"But there was nothing back there."

"There has to be," I said. "We have to go back."

Jack turned the car around and drove back slowly. When we reached the spot on the map, I told him to stop again. I got out and looked. There was nothing there but trees, bushes, and shrubbery. And water. Water on each side of the road.

"They're not here," Jack said as he came out to me.

A lot of words came to me involving Sherlock and no…but I held it back. This was no time to be witty or even provocative. I felt the panic knocking again. It threatened to overpower me.

"It can't be," I said. "The map says she's here, look. She should be here with her phone."

Jack took in a deep breath. "Or maybe…" he turned around and then ran toward a row of trees. "Stay here."

He almost disappeared in between the trees; then everything went eerily quiet.

"Jack?"

He didn't answer, so I tried again, this time slightly more nervous. "Jack? Where did you go? Did you find anything?"

The officers from the other cars came up to me.

"Where did he go?" one of them asked.

I shrugged. "In there somewhere."

There was a sound on their radios, and they immediately started to run toward where Jack had disappeared. My heart stood still as I heard them yelling, and then turmoil followed.

What the heck is going on?

My knees felt weak as I stood there, staring, wondering exactly what they were doing, or more importantly, what they had found.

Was it their bodies?

Stop it, Rebekka. You can't do this to yourself.

I then decided I'd be damned if I was just going to stand there and let fear and paranoia overtake me. I decided to disobey Jacks' order and rushed toward the trees. At first, I couldn't see what it was they were looking at, but as I came closer, I soon realized—in terror —exactly what it was.

A yellow school bus, half sunk into the river.

CHAPTER NINETEEN

May 2018

I turned to look at Jack Ryder. He was staring at the brown water, looking paralyzed. I didn't even think about it twice. I threw my phone in the grass, took off my shoes, and dove in. As the murky water surrounded me, I could hear Jack screaming at me, calling my name, but it was too late.

I swam deep into the water, toward the front of the sunken bus. As soon as I reached a window, I tried to look inside, but couldn't see anything through the dark glass. I tried to pull it open, but it was impossible. I continued to the next window, trying to push it, then swam for the door. It was locked, but I managed to find the outside hatch that opened it. Except it didn't work. It was stuck. I hammered my fists into the door, desperately wondering if my poor daughter was somewhere in there, fighting for her life, maybe already dead.

Were we too late? Had they all drowned?

The thought was unbearable, and I had to restrain myself to save the air I had left in my lungs when I suddenly noticed that one of the windows was cracked. I swam to it, clenched my fist, then punched the glass till it shattered. Blood floated in the water from the cut in my hand, but the window was open. I removed any small pieces of glass, so I wouldn't cut myself further, then grabbed the edges of the window and pulled myself inside.

Desperately, I looked around me, but I couldn't see much in the murky water. There was no one in the seat I had landed in and, as I reached the aisle of the bus, I couldn't see anyone there either.

Julie? Are you here, Julie?

I searched the seats, one after another, then the floors beneath and the entire aisle, but I found no kids, much to my relief. I swam one last time up and down the aisle and sensed I was about to run out of air. I headed for the window when there was movement behind me, and I paused. I turned around and saw something move in the water, fast. It swam past me once underneath me, then once above me, and my heart started to pound as I spotted its long tail slithering in the water behind it.

It was a gator.

Frantically, I whimpered, then grabbed for the window and pulled myself through it when something grabbed my leg and a huge pain shot through my body. I screamed but tried to keep my mouth closed and save the last bit of air I had left. I looked down and realized the gator had its jaws clenched around my thigh and it was pulling on me forcefully. I held onto the edge of the window, then turned to face the animal. I stared directly into the creature's black eyes. Blood was gushing into the water, floating slowly toward the surface.

I stared at the gator, desperately trying to get it to let go of my thigh, punching its jaws with my fists, but nothing helped. The gator kept pulling at me, trying to drag me further down, and I was out of air. My lungs screamed to be able to breathe, and it felt like a burning pain in them. That was when I remembered something I had once seen on TV about a gator hunter who told what he would do if one ever attacked him. I reached out two of my fingers, then poked each of them into one nostril of the gator, making sure I jammed them up so far that the creature could no longer breathe through its nose.

In order to not suffocate, the gator had to let go of my thigh, and so it did, but it was too late. I looked up at the light and tried to swim toward it, but I had no more strength left and no more air. I felt dizzy, and soon I couldn't stay conscious anymore. I felt myself slide toward the bottom, everything inside of me screaming to swim for the surface, but no parts of my body obeying anymore. I was barely awake when I felt someone grab me from behind.

CHAPTER TWENTY

May 2018

"What the heck were you thinking!"

I blinked my eyes as my sight slowly came back and the face staring into mine went from just a blur to a full person.

"J-Jack?"

His nostrils were flaring, his cheeks blushing red. "Why? Why would you throw yourself into the water like that? It's filled with gators. Don't you know anything?"

I coughed. I realized I was lying in the muddy grass next to the river. Jack's long hair was dripping on my face.

"You came in after me?"

"I had to…" he sighed and removed a lock of hair from his face. "You're crazy. Has anyone ever told you that?"

"I'm just a mother," I said and coughed again. My lungs were still burning, and it felt like I couldn't breathe properly. My leg was hurting crazily, and I looked down at the bloody bite.

"We called for an ambulance. You need that looked at," he said. "Lie still, please."

I smiled, and he gave me a look.

"She wasn't there," I said. "There were no kids down there.

They must have put them on another bus or something. That's good news, right? Means they're still alive, right?"

He took in a deep breath. "Yes, well…that is the good news. But I could have found that out without you getting yourself hurt."

"I couldn't very well just stand there and watch. What if she was down there?" I asked.

He gave me half a smile. "I guess I would probably have done the same had it been my kids," he said. "But that doesn't mean that it was a good idea. It was a terrible idea, Rebekka. I knew I should never have brought you here. It was a bad idea from the beginning."

I sat up. My head was spinning, but it felt better to sit than to lie down, so I did. A team of divers had arrived, and one of them was bringing something up from the water. It looked like a basket. He gave it to Jack, who looked down in it, then showed it to me. It was packed with cellphones and watches. I recognized Julie's phone as the one on top. I grabbed it and pressed a button. It was still turned on.

"Long live waterproof phones, right?" I said with a scoff.

Jack squatted next to me. "Hey, at least it brought us this far."

I nodded. He was right. I had hoped I would bring back my daughter and it was devastating that I still didn't know where she was or when I was going to see her again, but at least we had found the bus. And at least we hadn't found her dead body.

"So, I guess we're back to square, right?"

He cleared his throat. "It's back to square *one*, and no. Not completely. We've got the bus and the phones. We have evidence. And with evidence, we can begin an investigation. But let me do the dangerous work from now on, promise?"

I really couldn't.

I heard sirens in the distance and spotted the ambulance as it approached. Jack told me to stay still till they came for me, that I had lost a lot of blood. I did feel dizzy, so I laid myself back down, my heart still crushed and worried.

Where are you, Julie? Will I ever see you and hold you again?

CHAPTER TWENTY-ONE

May 2018

They drove for what felt like forever. At first, the road they drove on was smooth and normal, but later it turned bumpy, and the girls were jostled around inside the van. Julie held onto Alicia and the little girl that had clung to Julie ever since she had helped her earlier. She was crying helplessly, and Julie tried to calm her down.

"What's your name?" she asked.

The girl sniffled. It was terribly dark inside the van, but she could still see the girl's big eyes.

"Nikki."

"Okay, Nikki. My name is Julie. I'm in sixth grade; what grade are you in?" Julie asked, trying to make the girl feel better, even though she was about to scream in panic herself.

"First," she said.

"First grade, huh? And who's your teacher?"

Nikki sniffled again and wiped her right eye. "Mrs. Hall."

"I see. And do you like Mrs. Hall?"

"Yes. She's really nice."

The van started to bump really badly, and some kids screamed in the back. Julie held onto Nikki with both hands, so she wouldn't fly up and leaned on Alicia to try and hold her steady as well. Luckily, Julie was pretty heavy since she was so tall for her age. Haley wasn't so lucky. She was thrown up in the air, then bumped into the side of the van with a loud scream. Emmy from fifth grade helped her back up. Haley cried as she realized she was bleeding from her temple. The bumping continued, and it felt like every organ inside Julie's body was about to be shaken loose. She closed her eyes, praying it would stop soon, but it didn't. They had to be driving across a field or some terrain where there were no roads. Julie guessed they were staying off the roads in order not to be found by the police. They had to be looking for them by now.

They'll find you; don't worry, Julie. Just keep calm; just keep calm. If the police don't find you, your mom will. She won't stop till she does. You know her, Julie. You know how she is.

Julie opened her eyes as the bumping subsided a little. She was anxious about where they were going. If they kept going through places where there were no roads, it was going to take longer for the police to find them. With every bump, she felt like she was getting farther and farther away from her mother, and the thought terrified her to the core.

"What's your teacher's name?" Nikki asked, her voice shaking as the bumping grew worse again.

"W-what's that?" Julie asked.

"Y-your teacher? What's her name?"

Julie looked down at the little girl with the curly hair. "I have Mrs. Cherup. She's really nice. You might have her too one..." the bumping grew worse again, and Julie closed her eyes. Nikki shrieked and hid her face in Julie's lap. Alicia clung to her shoulder. Julie could hardly stand any more jostling. Someone else was hurt in the back and screamed.

Please be over soon. Please stop driving.

For a second, Julie actually thought God had heard them as the van came to a sudden halt. She let out a deep sigh of relief just as the door was pulled open and a bright light shone into their eyes and almost blinded them.

CHAPTER TWENTY-TWO

October 1991

J ane got out of bed by swinging her legs out over the edge first, then sitting up before sliding to the ground, holding a hand underneath her growing stomach. She was getting big, really big. But that wasn't such a strange thing since the scan earlier in her pregnancy had shown that she was, in fact, carrying twins.

She put her tired feet on the carpet, then rose up and walked—no make that waddled because that's how it felt and looked—to the bathroom. Jane was nervous about the prospect of having to give birth, twice, but mostly about how her life would turn out afterward. Everyone told her having twins was tough, and she wasn't sure she was completely prepared for it. But then again, was anyone ever really prepared for having a child? Was it that much different having two? Did you ever really know what you were getting into when giving birth to your first one?

That was how her co-worker and mother of three boys had laid it out for her. You never knew. Even if you had done it before, you were never fully prepared. That was part of the charm, if you wanted to call it that, she said. The loss of control. No matter what spat out of you in that hospital bed, it was bound to change your life and you forever.

"Doesn't matter if it's the first or the tenth if you ask me. Every one of them is different, and they don't come with no manual."

Jane had, however, gotten herself a manual. She had gotten herself five of them. Five books on how to raise a baby and she read them intently every night before bedtime, making sure not to miss any part of them so that nothing would be a surprise to her.

Jane didn't like surprises.

Jane waddled out of the bathroom and into her walk-in closet and took out a dress. She pulled it over her head, but it was way too tight around her stomach, and she took it off, then hung it back up. She tried another one, then another, then grabbed her maternity pants that she had been wearing for three days in a row now. She only had that one pair, and she was sick of wearing them every day.

She missed working already and regretted having to quit so shortly after she got pregnant. She had asked Bob if she couldn't wait till she was about to give birth, like a month in advance, but Bob wouldn't hear of it. She didn't understand why she had to walk around the house, big and bored beyond anything, waiting for these babies to come out. Why couldn't she just work a little? She wanted to enjoy these last months out in the world.

Looking at her pants in the mirror, she was reminded that she hadn't shopped in months. Bob took care of their finances now, which was only fair since he was the one who made all the money, and besides, she shouldn't *worry herself with that*, but that also meant she didn't have anything to shop for or to spend on herself anymore.

She stared at her own reflection, then found a shirt that was just big enough to fit around her stomach, but it stuck out in an unorderly way, and Jane sighed deeply. She used to be so neat and always fashionable. Now, she just looked like a big fat bag of potatoes.

She walked down the stairs, holding onto the railing, panting and wheezing. She couldn't believe she still had two and a half months to go. How big was her stomach going to get?

Bob had made pancakes and bacon for her. Jane sat in a chair and began to eat. She was so incredibly hungry, but she couldn't eat much at a time because the babies took up so much space. Usually, she would have to eat again in about an hour or so. She watched as Bob ate and sipped coffee, jealously missing the caffeine. But Bob had told her it wasn't good for the babies, so she had stayed away from it all through the pregnancy.

"I made you some tea," he said, smiling. "Green tea, no caffeine. Should help with the swelling of your feet."

She smiled back, holding a hand over her stomach. "I noticed. Thank you, sweetie."

Jane sipped it and ate some bacon, crunching it. The babies kicked inside her stomach and she made a strained face. It was fun and exciting in the beginning, but now it was getting uncomfortable.

"Are they kicking again?" Bob asked and put his hand on her stomach. Then he laughed, as what they guessed was a heel or maybe an elbow poked out underneath the tight skin and moved across her stomach.

"I can't wait to see my babies," Bob said with a grin. He took Jane's hand in his. "We're going to be a real family. Just the four of us, no one else. A real family, Jane. It's what I've wanted all of my life. A family with a mom and a dad."

Jane sighed. She knew this was all he wanted. They had both grown up with single moms and no dads, so that was her wish too. She wanted a family; she really did. Only she still wondered if they were too young.

"Here, let me get you some more orange juice," he said. He got up, pulled a chair out, and helped her to get her feet up on it. She smiled. Bob was so incredibly considerate, always putting her needs before his. She sure was a lucky woman to be with him.

"I was thinking that maybe I could get some money, so I could buy myself some new clothes?" she asked, cautiously.

She hated asking Bob for money. It wasn't often she did since he took care of the grocery shopping, and everything else for that matter, so she could focus on being pregnant.

"I don't have anything to wear that I like anymore," she said. "I would like to get a nice dress."

Bob stopped pouring the juice into her glass. He slammed the fridge shut, hard.

"And just why is that, might I ask?"

"Because I look so ugly in these same clothes that I wear every day."

He stood with the glass in his hand, then approached her, his jaw clenched. "And who is it exactly that you have to look *oh-so-pretty* for, huh?"

Jane blinked. She had no idea what he was talking about. "What do you mean?"

"I mean who is it that you're making yourself look good for, huh?"

"You. Who else?"

"I think you look perfectly fine the way you are," he said. "So, it can't be me. It can't be for my sake."

"Who else would it be? You're the only one I see all day, Bob. I want to look good because it makes me feel better about myself, and hopefully, you'll like it too. Geez. Why are you so insecure?"

And just like that, it was like she flipped a switch. Bob took the glass and threw it through the air, hitting the wall behind her, shattering the glass. Orange juice was smeared all over the wall and was running down it in stripes. Jane rose to her feet in fear, but she didn't move fast enough. Bob was in front of her. He lifted his fist and slammed it into her face so hard, she fell onto the tiles.

CHAPTER TWENTY-THREE

May 2018

I was quite high on pain medication by the time I was taken home from the hospital. Jack drove me since Sune had to stay with the kids and since he couldn't drive yet. He had regained about eighty percent of the mobility in his legs, but he couldn't count on them. Not enough to drive a car.

Jack opened the door to the car and lifted me up into his arms. He carried me inside and carefully put me on the couch.

"Thanks, man," Sune said and placed a hand on Jack's shoulder. "She told me on the phone how you saved her life."

"No problem," Jack said and looked at me with his head tilted. "Now promise me you'll stay out of trouble. I can't spend all my time rescuing you."

I smiled, hazed. "I ain't making no promises."

"All right. I have to get back to work," Jack said, shifting on his feet. "I'll be in touch."

He left, and Sune sat down in the chair next to me, letting go of his walker. He sighed and grabbed my hand in his.

"You scared me today," he said.

I nodded. "I was scared too. Of losing Julie. Heck, I still am, terrified." I felt tears pile up in my eyes. "Where is she, Sune? What have they done to her? It's all dark out; why isn't she home yet?"

"I'm sure she'll be home."

"It's late, Sune. Do I have to go through an entire night without her? How? How am I supposed to do that?"

Sune leaned over and hugged me. My leg was still hurting, despite the pain medication.

"M-mom?"

William came out of the bedroom, rubbing his eyes. Then his face lit up. "Is Ju-Ju home?"

Sune got up. "No, buddy. You should be sleeping."

I grabbed Sune's shirt and stopped him by pulling it. "It's okay.

I looked at my son and reached out my hands.

"Hi there, buddy. Are you gonna come and give your mom a hug?"

William waddled toward me and threw himself on top of me. I hugged him tightly, trying to push all the thoughts of devastation and catastrophe back in my mind. Tears rolled across my cheeks as I refused to let go of him. Finally, he pushed himself up and looked at my leg.

"Gator!" he said.

"Yes, buddy. Gator bit Mommy right there in the thigh."

Tobias had come down the stairs too and approached me. "Did it hurt?" he asked, looking at my leg.

I nodded. "Pretty bad."

"Did you have to have stitches?"

I nodded. "Come see."

He looked at my leg, then shuddered.

"I know," I said. "It looks terrible, all swollen and pink, but it should be all right, they say. I'll have a scar, though."

"Coool," William said.

"I guess it is pretty cool. I'll have a cool story to tell, right?" I sniffled. "At least, I hope so."

William saw the tears pile up again, then kissed my cheek. "Ju-Ju will be home soon," he said. "Pinky-promise."

I chuckled and wiped away my tears. "Pinky promise, huh? You know those are unbreakable, right?"

He looked very confident. "Yes."

CHAPTER TWENTY-FOUR

May 2018

They were being kept in a small shack. A couple of hours later, the door was opened, and they were told to come out. It was dark outside. Julie held Alicia and Nikki close as they followed the gunmen across the dusty ground, leaving the small shack behind.

Julie felt such a deep fear rise in her. She had thought the shack was where they were going to keep them, and she hadn't been looking forward to that since there was no AC and it had been very hot for all of them. But now, as they walked toward what appeared to be nothing…no houses, no buildings, no civilization, she began to fear that the shack had been the better choice.

"Where are we going?" Alicia asked.

"I don't know," Julie said. "Just do as they say."

"I want my mommy," Nikki sniffled. She was exhausted and couldn't stop crying. Julie felt a thickness in her throat too but held it back. She had to be strong for the little ones. They needed her.

"I know," she whispered. "I want my mommy too. I'm sure we'll see them soon, okay?"

The gunmen stopped in the middle of a rocky area, then pointed in front of them with their guns.

"Get in."

Julie looked but couldn't see anything there. Then she watched as the first two girls in the front of the line seemed to descend into the ground.

"I have to pee," Nikki complained. "Real bad."

"Be quiet," one of the gunmen said.

"She has to pee," Julie said. "I think we all do. We haven't had a bathroom break for hours. Most of the kids have done it in their pants."

"Be quiet," the gunman said again.

"But…"

"I said, be quiet."

"She has to pee really bad. You can't treat us like this!"

"BE QUIET!"

Julie stopped talking. She stared at the man in front of her. The gun was pointing at her, placed closed to her face. Julie was hardly breathing as she stared down the barrel.

The line moved, and Julie lowered her head, then moved with the line. The gunman moved away. Julie wiped a tear from her cheek, then continued, her heart throbbing in her chest, more tears running down her cheeks. She focused on keeping her breathing calm and not panicking as they approached the hole in the ground where all the girls had disappeared.

One by one, the girls climbed down a ladder and into what appeared to be a big box truck, covered under several feet of dirt. After the last girl had entered, the gunmen removed the ladder and closed the hatch above them.

Julie stared for a long time at the point where they had come inside, then sat down, heavily sweating. She pulled Alicia and Nikki close while whispering comforting words into their ears:

"This is just where we're going to spend the night. That's all. Don't you worry now. Don't you worry."

CHAPTER TWENTY-FIVE

October 1991

"**E**verything looks perfect. Your babies are in perfect health as far as we can see."

Jane looked at Bob who was standing next to her while the doctor took off his gloves. Bob was holding her hand and had been all through the ultrasound. She had felt him squeeze hers when he heard the babies' heartbeats. Bob insisted on being there for all of Jane's doctor's visits now, and she figured that was perfectly normal since he needed to know everything too.

"That's wonderful; so we shouldn't be nervous about the pain she has felt?" Bob asked.

"It's only natural that she might feel contractions. They're called Braxton Hicks contractions and are perfectly harmless."

"Phew," he said and looked at Jane again.

"You have absolutely nothing to worry about," the doctor said. He stood for a second and looked at Jane, then took in a deep breath. "Do you mind me asking where you got that bruise?"

Jane felt her body go cold. She had tried to cover it up, using plenty of foundation, but apparently not well enough.

"Oh, that," Bob said, looking down at Jane. "Funny story, Doctor. See…it's all my fault."

Jane looked up at him. She had never thought he would say that. Bob had apologized endlessly after hitting her to the floor that day, and she had promised to forgive him. Since then, he had showered her with flowers and chocolate, and he had even cooked dinner for her every night so she wouldn't have to stand up so much. He had been the sweetest most considerate man, and she didn't want him to get into trouble for losing his temper like that. It was, after all, only this once. He had promised it would never happen again and she believed he would never do that to himself or to her again. He messed up. Everyone was allowed to make a mistake, right?

"It is?" the doctor asked, putting his papers down. He took off his glasses and looked up at Bob. "How so?"

"Well, the thing is…God, I am such an idiot. You see, I'm in the kitchen, cooking, right? And in comes Jane, right? I don't hear her, and so I open the cabinet and slam the door right into her face. Clumsy me. I feel terrible, though."

He clenched her hand and held it to his heart, looking at her sadly. The doctor seemed to be scrutinizing them both. Jane felt her heart pounding in her chest, then forced a smile.

"It was just as much my fault," she said, taking in a deep, ragged breath. "For sneaking up on you like that."

"Will you listen to her, Doctor?" Bob said. "Isn't she just the best wife in the world?"

The doctor smiled, relieved, and nodded. "I'm sure she is. And she will soon become a mother of not just one but two children. That is quite the accomplishment. I am happy to hear that you're treating her well and cooking for her. She's gonna need all the care she can get in the last months of the pregnancy. I'm happy she's in such good hands."

CHAPTER TWENTY-SIX

May 2018

I can't say I slept much, if at all. I stayed on the couch all night, the phone clutched in my hand, staring at it, constantly pressing the button to make sure it was still on, hoping and praying for it to ring and bring me good news. I was waiting for just a voice, no matter whose, telling me she was on her way home, that they had found her and were going to bring her to me.

It must have been the longest night of my life. All I could think of was Julie and how she was doing and whether she was safe. Was she thirsty? Was she hungry? Did she get anything to eat? What did those people—whoever they were—want with her? What did they want from us? A ransom?

As soon as the sun came up, I dialed Jack's number. I couldn't wait any longer and had to have the latest news.

"Rebekka," he said, sounding as tired as I felt.

"Please, tell me you have news."

"We found Mrs. Baker," he said. "She was brought in late last night. She had been visiting her son in Ocala, she said, so that's why she hadn't answered her phone."

"So, what does she say?" I asked.

"Well, you know I can't reveal any details, but I can tell you that she says she didn't see or hear Mr. Meckler tell the kids to go on another bus, but that it had to have been him since he was the only one out there with her. And she didn't even know about the other bus."

"And what does Mr. Meckler say about that?" I asked.

"We're still questioning him, so that's what we're going to find out hopefully soon. But so far, he's sticking to his story. He says she had to have been the one to tell the kids to go on another bus since he didn't do it. But he didn't exactly hear her say it."

I sighed. This was annoying. If they were just accusing one another, then we were getting nowhere.

"But who is right, then? Isn't there anyone who can tell us who is lying? There were a ton of kids there? Didn't they see or hear anything?" I asked, then thought about Tobias, who hadn't seen much. He was busy talking to his friends, he said.

"We'll have to go talk to more of them today," he said. "But so far, there have been two kids telling us that Mr. Meckler grabbed Haley and told her to get out of the line."

"Well, there you go; he's lying then," I said.

"But…the second kid also says that Haley was told to go get her lunchbox, and he saw her walk inside, then come back out."

"So, what does that mean?"

Jack sighed. "I don't know. But it does support Meckler's story."

I groaned. "And while they fight over that, the girls are out there somewhere desperate to come home. They must be terrified by now. I know I am."

"You and me both, Rebekka," Jack said. "You and me both."

CHAPTER TWENTY-SEVEN

May 2018

I t was unbearably hot inside the buried box truck. Julie hardly slept at all that night and, when she woke up, she felt like throwing up. The kidnappers had placed boxes inside, made from plywood, and they had carved a small hole on top of them, so the girls could use them as toilets, but the smell started to spread, and in the hot moist air, it soon became almost impossible to breathe properly.

Next to the toilets, the kidnappers had stacked food. Several boxes of cereal, a jar of peanut butter, and a pack of bread, a couple of boxes of crackers along with bottles of water. Julie grabbed a water and some crackers but ate mainly because she knew she had to in order to survive. Not because she had an appetite.

She handed bottles of water to Alicia and Nikki and gave them some crackers as well, but only Alicia drank and ate. Nikki sat in the corner, her knees pulled up under her chin, rocking back and forth, sobbing.

Julie drank greedily from the water while staring at the food piled up and the mattresses scattered on the floor.

How long are they planning on keeping us?

Judging by the amount of food and water, she guessed it had to be a very long time.

Realizing this, Julie almost choked on the water she was gulping down. In the back of the box truck, Haley threw up, and a girl whimpered in deep fear. No one was speaking; everyone was just trying to get through the next few minutes without panicking, without losing it completely.

The worst part was the feeling that there wasn't enough air. Simply thinking about it would get to her, and she held a hand to her throat, feeling like she was suffocating.

Julie sat down on a mattress close to Alicia, gasping for air, and fighting to keep the panic at bay. The mattress was dirty, and there were bugs crawling on top of it. A drop of sweat left her forehead and clung to her eyebrow for a few seconds before it gave up and fell to her arm. She stared at the drop, wondering how long it would stay there before it would dry out. It didn't last long in the heat before it was gone.

Julie closed her eyes for a few seconds, remembering her room at the pink house on the beach. How she missed her bed there and her blanket and pillow. How she longed to breathe the fresh ocean air again or just be able to go to the toilet without having to do it in front of nine others. She leaned her head to the side and remembered her mother. The thought caused a violent pinch in her stomach. She missed her so much. She thought about her younger brother, William, and her stepbrother, Tobias, and imagined them playing together in the pool. Oh, the nice, cool pool. What she wouldn't give to be back there now and not buried several feet underground.

"It's a coffin," she mumbled to herself as she opened her eyes again. "They made us a giant coffin and buried us."

CHAPTER TWENTY-EIGHT

June 1992

The babies were a blessing. From the moment they came into their lives, Bob and Jane had never been happier. It was like it all came together, like this was what they were meant to do...being parents.

Bob was good and helped Jane out as much as he possibly could. He would even get up at night when one of them woke up. More often than not, it was both of them since when once one started to cry, the other would chime in a few seconds later.

He changed their diapers and always had an available hand to hold one of them when Jane was tired from breastfeeding. It was exhausting having two at the same time, but it was also so incredibly fulfilling in many ways. The love of the two little girls brought the two of them so close together; they soon seemed to forget everything that had gone before this moment. It was like they had started completely over from scratch.

After six months, however, things turned. It began with a phone call from Bob's brother one Saturday afternoon, telling him that Bob's sister, Irene, had died. A heart attack in the middle of the night, they said. The shock of losing his sister so suddenly made

Bob lose it. He sat down on a chair in the living room. He was staring into thin air when Jane came in.

"Are you all right? Bob? Who was that?"

He looked at her. She put both babies in a playpen and sighed, exhausted, while Bob said:

"That was Jim."

"Your brother? What did he want?"

Bob rose to his feet. Jane saw that something had changed in his eyes. Something was different and frightening.

"What's it to you? What do you care anyway?"

"I'm sorry," she said and looked away.

"You don't care about me, do you? I'm just your little errand boy, am I right?"

"Bob…what's gotten into…?"

"What do you do all day while I'm at work, huh? You screw that neighbor. Don't you think for one second that I haven't seen how you look at him."

Jane turned her head and looked at Bob. She had no idea who he was even talking about.

"What neighbor? I don't even go out. I'm at home all day taking care of our children."

"Ah, don't give me that."

"Excuse me? Don't give you what?" she asked.

As she said the words, she immediately knew she shouldn't have. She could tell by the fire in Bob's eyes that she had overstepped a line. She had made him angry.

Bob grabbed her by the throat and pressed her up against the wall behind her, smashing her against it so hard she lost the hearing in one ear temporarily. He was choking her now, and Jane was desperately fighting for her life. Somehow, she managed to kick him in the stomach, and he let go of her. Dizzy, she got up to her feet and ran for the phone, but Bob was quickly on top of her, grabbing the phone and smashing it to the ground. He then slammed his fist into her face over and over again, continuing for so long that Jane lost consciousness before he let go of her. Sweat and saliva dripped from his chin as he stood above her.

"Now look at what you made me do. Look at you! Will you never learn?"

CHAPTER TWENTY-NINE
May 2018

It was a dark and cloudy day. One of the rare ones in Florida, the Sunshine State. It wasn't raining, though, so we still sat outside in the heat while eating breakfast. I liked looking out over the ocean. It calmed me down. Sune had placed me in a chair and Tobias had given me another chair for my leg, so I could keep it up. I wasn't supposed to move around today at all, but I didn't want to miss out on breakfast on the porch with my family. My phone lying in front of me kept buzzing with Amber Alerts for the ten missing girls and, every time I heard the sound, it made my heart sink.

I barely had any appetite since all I could think about was Julie, but I still forced myself to eat some of Sune's scrambled eggs and bacon that he had so caringly made for us.

Tobias was pushing his eggs around on the plate. I sent him a smile, hoping to cheer him up a little, but it didn't help. I could tell he was fighting to keep himself from breaking down and crying. Heck, I was too. Only William seemed to be able to eat, even with everything that was going on. He shoveled in his eggs, then asked for more.

I drank some coffee while Sune served our youngest and he dug in once again. The boy always had a good appetite, I had to give him that. I couldn't stop staring at him. Somehow, it cheered me up to watch him eat. When he was done, I looked out over the ocean again. The heavy clouds matched my mood perfectly.

I felt a hand in mine and looked down to see William. He had left his chair and come up to me. I pulled him up into my lap, and we looked at the dark clouds together.

"The clouds kind of look angry, don't you think?" I asked.

He gave it a thoughtful look, then said: "The clouds may be angry but not angry enough to cry."

I chuckled and hugged my poetic son. "True. Doesn't look like rain, just lots of gloomy weather."

"I wanna play ball," William said and let himself slide to the ground. He ran into the grass and grabbed the soccer ball I had bought for him. He started to run with it, then kicked it in between the two palm trees we had pretended to mark the goal.

"Goal!" he yelled and looked at me triumphantly. I chuckled again. I looked at my phone on the table. I was sick of waiting for it to ring, but still, I couldn't help myself.

I felt Sune's hand as he placed it on top of mine.

"You want more coffee?" he asked as I turned to look at him.

I nodded. "Yes, please. I need it today."

He leaned over and kissed me. I was so happy that he was in progress and that all his bitterness toward the world was gone. He was back to being my happy Sune, my sweet, caring, happy Sune, who—even though he was slightly younger than me—always carried my every burden.

He looked into my eyes. "We'll get her home."

I sighed. "You know she would have loved this weather, right?"

He scoffed and nodded. "I'll get you that coffee."

CHAPTER THIRTY

May 2018

A licia was throwing up too now, and Julie could barely restrain herself from doing it as well while listening to the sounds of her losing the contents of her stomach. Many kids were crying, calling for their mothers, and the heat was making the air thick.

Julie tried for hours to be strong for the little ones, but even she had her limits to what she could bear. The stench was agonizing.

"This is it," Alicia said when she was done throwing up, and she laid down on the dirty mattress. "They're not coming for us. They don't care. They're just going to let us die down here, aren't they?"

Julie wanted to say something; she wanted to be the one to comfort them all and tell them everything was going to be all right, that, of course, they wouldn't just let them suffocate and die down here, that the police would come, their parents would come, or the kidnappers would come and show mercy on them. But she couldn't find the words to say it.

Julie looked at Nikki, who was sitting with her head leaned against the side of the box. She hadn't said a word for at least an hour and wasn't even crying anymore. Suddenly, Julie missed her constant crying and calling for her mother.

"Nikki?" she said and reached out her hand toward her. But the girl didn't react.

Julie got up and staggered to her, then pulled her shoulder. "Nikki?"

The girl fell backward into her arms.

"NIKKI!"

Julie felt her forehead. "Oh, my God, she's burning up. She's sick. Nikki, wake up. Please, Nikki."

Julie asked Alicia to bring her some water. Alicia helped Nikki drink a little, but most of it spilled onto the floor.

"Is she…?" Alicia asked.

Julie shook her head. "No. She's still breathing."

A new wave of panic erupted inside Julie. Was this the way it was going to be? One after another, they were going to cave in?

"Please, Nikki. Please, drink some water," she said, then grabbed the bottle and placed it on Nikki's lips. She poured some in and soon Nikki was drinking. Julie breathed a sigh of relief when there was a sound from above them, and the metal plate that the kidnappers had closed was pulled aside, and a wave of fresh air came in. All the kids ran to the opening and gasped for air, taking in every last bit of it.

A figure showed up in the opening, and they all screamed and pulled away. A ladder then came down, and someone stepped inside. It was one of the kidnappers. He was still wearing pantyhose over his face.

"Hey," Julie yelled and walked toward him, still holding Nikki in her arms. "She's sick. Please, help her."

The man looked at Nikki, then shook his head. "Not her." He turned around and spotted Alondra sitting on one of the mattresses.

"That one."

CHAPTER THIRTY-ONE
May 2018

"It's a nightmare, Rebekka. People are coming in from everywhere."

Jack sounded used up on the phone. I couldn't blame him. It was late in the afternoon before I called him again and I felt pretty good about myself for waiting so long. It took all my strength to not constantly bother him for news. But as the day went by and evening approached, I was beginning to fear that I would have to go through yet another night without my daughter.

The thought was excruciating.

Sue and Nancy had both been over for a few hours earlier, and we had tried to talk each other up and not let fear get the better of us, but, boy, it was hard to do. Close to impossible. Especially when you know that in cases of child disappearances, the first twenty-four hours were so crucial in the chances of finding them again.

"Investigators and reporters have flown in from all over the country, turning the town into a frenzy," Jack said. "Even the city council is all over it. This thing has hit Cocoa Beach like a freight train. And those poor parents. It's getting to me; it really is."

"Did they find anything on the bus?" I asked.

"All we know is that the bus was stolen from a local school down in Melbourne eighteen months ago. Since it was submerged under water, there are no fingerprints or anything we can get from it."

"And what about Mrs. Baker and Mr. Meckler? Are you getting anywhere with them?" I asked.

"I'm afraid not. The FBI is here and has taken over the interrogations. But they haven't been able to get any closer to the truth than we have. I am sorry, Rebekka. I wish I had better news. We have search teams out everywhere, especially focused on the area around where we found the bus. They are searching with dogs and helicopters, and all the police in the entire state are on high alert looking for these girls. Plus, it's all over the news. We are doing all we can."

"But sometimes that even isn't enough," I mumbled and looked at William who was doing a puzzle in the living room. The clouds had finally been angry enough to rain, and now I heard thunder as well.

"Where the heck can you even hide ten kids?" I asked, shattered. "Without being seen?"

"I know. It seems impossible. It's like they have vanished from the surface of the earth."

"So, you say they stole the bus eighteen months ago, huh?" I said. "Guess they've been planning it for a long time. You think they did this for a ransom?"

"It's possible," he said, "since most of the girls come from wealthy families and several of them live in beach houses. It might be why they targeted this bus route because there are a lot of wealthy kids."

"Just doesn't explain why they only took the girls," I said. "And no boys."

"True. Maybe they are easier to control."

"Then they don't know my daughter very well; that's for sure," I said with a scoff.

Jack went absent for a second, and I could hear someone speaking to him in the background. I wasn't sure, but I thought I heard that person say, "We just received a tip you need to look at."

My heart started to pound.

"I need to go, Rebekka," he said.

"Of course. Of course."

Then we hung up, but this time I felt a pinch of hope emerge inside me, a feeling I hadn't had for many hours.

They had a tip.

CHAPTER THIRTY-TWO

June 1999

J ane kept getting pregnant in the following years, and when the twins were seven years old, she had her fifth child, the first boy. Bob was excited to have a boy finally, but things between them weren't the same anymore. He still hit her from time to time, and she had learned how to live with it, and how to hide it should anyone come to visit. She loved the children. They were her entire life. They were all she had. All she lived for.

Jane never left the house much since Bob didn't want her to, and she didn't want to face people being bruised and answer questions. She had even stopped seeing her mother, telling her they were busy whenever she asked to see her grandbabies. Most of her life was spent taking care of the children and making sure Bob was kept happy.

When the little boy, Matthew, was three months old, Bob came home from work one day in the middle of the day. He walked into the living room where Jane was sitting on the couch. She was breast-feeding while the four girls were all running around and screaming.

Seeing him come in, she put the baby down, even though he wasn't done eating. She got up and walked to Bob.

"Why are you home now?"

"I was fired," he said and kicked a doll on the floor. Jane picked it up and started to clean up. The doll lost her arm when Bob kicked it and seeing this, their daughter, Anna, threw a tantrum. Throwing herself on the floor, she squealed and screamed that it was her favorite doll, and now it was ruined. Fearing Bob's reaction to this, Jane tried to comfort her, but that just made things worse. Anna yelled at her dad for kicking her doll, and her dad responded by slamming his fist into her nose. Much to her horror, Jane heard a crack as the nose broke. Jane screamed, and so did three-year-old Anna. Blood was gushing from her nose onto her face. Jane stood like she was paralyzed for a few seconds. Then she attacked Bob. She threw herself at him and started to hit him, but he was much stronger than her. He grabbed her arms and threw her to the ground. Then, towering above her, holding her down using his weight, he beat her. He beat her till she was so broken she couldn't even feel the punches anymore. But, worst of all, he did it in front of all the children and even called them to come out and watch while he did it, telling them this was what would happen *if you didn't behave properly*.

Then he left, slamming the door behind him.

Through curtains of blood, Jane made eye contact with one of the twins and told her to call for an ambulance. When the paramedics came, along with the police, they were all taken to the emergency room. Anna was treated for her broken nose, while it took Jane three days in bed to be able even to stand up again.

That was when she'd had enough.

Bob came to her in the hospital, carrying flowers and balloons. He told her he was never going to do anything like this again and he promised things would be different, just as he had so many times before. But this time, Jane wasn't buying it. She was going to leave him, she told him, and he would never see her again. When he cried and told her he loved her and that he couldn't live without her, she simply answered:

"What kind of man loves like this?"

Little did she know that her struggles had only just begun.

CHAPTER THIRTY-THREE

May 2018

I was doing exactly what I wasn't supposed to, yet I couldn't help myself. I was watching the news over and over again, then reading about it online, about what they said about the mysterious disappearance of ten girls from Cocoa Beach. I knew it wasn't good for me since it only added to the fear and anxiety, especially the many speculations and so-called experts, but I had to do something while the rest of the house slept. I couldn't just go to sleep; I could find no rest.

Yet somehow, I must have dozed off because once I woke up again, it was light out. The sun was shining above the ocean and hitting my eyes. Gone were the dark clouds from the day before.

I blinked my eyes, then looked at the wound in my thigh. It was healing nicely already even though it was still swollen, but the pain was almost gone. I still popped a painkiller, then got up and managed to walk to the kitchen. I was limping, yes, but I was back to walking again and moving around on my own. It felt good. I made myself some coffee and enjoyed it while looking at the sunrise, savoring the last few minutes of quiet before William woke.

The coffee felt good, and soon I was fully awake when the door to William's room opened, and he came out, still in his PJs, looking all adorable with his unruly hair and rubbing his eyes.

"Morning, buddy. You sleep well?"

He nodded with a yawn and sat by the breakfast counter. I poured him some cereal. He ate it in silence, crunching loudly. I usually didn't like that sound much, but today, I enjoyed it. I liked that at least one of my kids was safe and getting something to eat.

"Is Ju-Ju home yet?" he asked.

I shook my head.

"Ah, man," he said. "She promised to go in the pool with me. Tobias never wants to."

"Maybe you and he can play soccer today?" I suggested. "Have him teach you that trick you like so much."

William sighed. "He doesn't want to."

"Maybe if you ask him again nicely, huh?"

I sipped my coffee and looked at my son. Then I grabbed some toast and buttered it, thinking I had to eat something to keep strong. It was so easy for me to forget to eat with all this going on. I wondered about my dad back in Denmark and whether he was all right. I hadn't called him and told him what had happened since he didn't need the worry. He had enough to deal with as it was.

"I'm gonna watch TV," William said.

"Okay, buddy."

He was supposed to go to his pre-school today, but Sune and I had decided to keep him at home while all this was going on. Tobias was home anyway since the school had closed while they searched for the girls. The entire town seemed to have shut down. It was like everyone was paralyzed, the other moms had told me when they stopped by the day before. Bars and restaurants had closed down, except for Juice N' Java that had somehow become a gathering place for police and townspeople. The owner made sandwiches for the search teams, and there was free coffee for everyone who needed it. I hadn't been down there myself, but I had seen in articles online how there were signs in the windows downtown with posters and pictures of the girls. Some had even written on plywood. BRING OUR GIRLS HOME!

I sighed and finished my coffee, then grabbed a refill before I walked out to the pool area and sat in a chair, putting my foot up on another chair to rest it a little.

I sat in the shade and stared at the cars and trucks driving by on A1A, listening to the steady music they made, and it came to me with a sudden vicious realization that the kidnappers who had taken my kid could be in one of them, simply passing by, chuckling as they went to town for whatever they needed. My kid could be hidden nearby, and there was no way I would ever know. The thought made me walk to the street and start staring at each and every car that passed me.

It was while I watched a huge moving truck pass me, thinking that could easily carry ten little girls, hiding them in the back, that I heard her scream.

CHAPTER THIRTY-FOUR
May 2018

The scream came from a couple of houses down. It was followed by a couple of deep groans and then more screams. They weren't normal screams like the ones you'd hear from kids in the pool or playing in the waves on the beach. No, this was different. These screams harbored deep anxiety inside of them, despair so profound it could only come from a mother who feared for the life of her child.

I hurried as fast as I could on my hurt leg toward the house and spotted Nancy in her driveway. She had sunk to her knees. In one hand, she held what looked like a piece of paper. On the ground in front of her lay an envelope that had contained the letter she had just gotten from her mailbox, only a few steps away.

"Nancy!" I said and limped closer. "What's wrong?"

I knelt next to her and ignored the pounding pain in my wounds. The look on Nancy's face made everything inside me want to scream. Never had I seen so much torment in a person's eyes, so much horror, such blackness covering her entire face.

Nancy couldn't speak. Instead, she held out her hand and showed me something. Even before I looked, I knew it was going to haunt me in my dreams for days to come; I just knew it. Yet I looked. Because I had to. I had to see the blood and the two fingers. I had to see the two small fingers that could only belong to a child, one carrying a ring Nancy had given her when she had been promoted from second grade because that's what people did these days. You celebrated the small victories every year when your child had survived yet another year of elementary school and not been run over by a bus or even shot by some sick kid who one morning woke up and decided today was the day to shoot everyone down.

"It came in the mail," Nancy said, almost wailing. Spit and saliva spurted out from her mouth and nose as she said the words. "This. This…"

Her hand quivering, she showed me the letter that only had one sentence:

Ten little Injuns standin' in a line.

I shook my head, not understanding any of it. "What's it supposed to mean?"

But Nancy was out of reach. She merely stared at the fingers, her lips shuddering.

"I…I can't…Alondra, my sweet, sweet Alondra," she said, then cried while touching one of the fingers lightly. She looked up, and our eyes met.

"She just had her nails done."

"We need to get you inside," I said and helped her up.

It wasn't easy, and the pain in my thigh was excruciating, yet I managed to ignore it and let Nancy rest on my shoulder while helping her back to the house. She was mumbling her daughter's name over and over again. Once we were inside the house and Nancy was put in a chair in the living room, I grabbed my phone and called Jack Ryder.

"You need to come, now."

CHAPTER THIRTY-FIVE

May 2018

A mob had gathered in front of the police station in downtown Cocoa Beach when we got there. We had spent hours at Nancy's house while the forensics team took care of the fingers and the letter and while a doctor came and gave Nancy an injection to calm her down. Her husband, Kyle, had come back from work after Jack called him and he was taking care of her. Jack had told him just to let her sleep. Jack had then asked me to come with him back to the station and give my testimony. Exactly how these people had known so quickly about what had happened, I had no explanation for, but it was a small town. News traveled fast here and, apparently, the rumor of the letter and the two fingers had beat us there because most of the people gathered outside the entrance were parents of the ten girls.

As soon as they spotted Jack Ryder, they addressed him, their faces angry and eyes torn in fear. I had borrowed one of Sune's crutches that he barely used anymore to support me.

"What are you going to do?" Emmy's dad asked and grabbed Jack by the shoulder.

"You have him in there, don't you?" Mary, Haley's mom asked. "You have Mr. Meckler."

Jack exhaled. "Now, let's not get ahead of ourselves…"

"Is it true her fingers were in the letter?" Mary continued. "They cut off her fingers?"

"What do they want?" Britney's mom, Jessica, asked. "A ransom? Because I'll give them anything if they'll just keep my daughter's fingers attached to her hand. I'll sell everything I have if need to."

Jack exhaled again. "We don't know yet. There have been no demands so far for a ransom."

"And the letter? Can you trace the letter?" a reporter asked. Her cameraman had been in Jacks' face while he spoke to the concerned parents, probably making excellent emotional TV the way they liked it. I knew how these people thought and suddenly felt ashamed for being one of them. It didn't feel good to be the one on the other side of it.

"We will try our best," Jack answered and tried to make his way through the crowd.

"Are you getting any answers out of Mr. Meckler yet?" Emmy's dad, John said. "You have my permission to torture him if needed."

A couple of the parents agreed and chimed in with a *yeah, give him whatever is needed,* or *do what it takes.*

Jack shook his head. "There will be no such thing. Besides, we don't even know if he is involved in any way so far."

"How can you be certain?" the reporter asked. "You've interviewed him several times since the kidnapping happened. Will you say that he had nothing to do with it or is he still your main suspect?"

"There'll be a news conference later on where we'll explain everything we can at this point in the investigation," Jack said, trying to get her off his back, but it didn't work.

"Would you say that you have no leads, then? No suspects? Or are you holding back from these poor parents trying to find out where their kids are?"

"No," Jack said shaking his head. I could tell he wasn't used to having the media in his face like this. "I am…we're doing all we can."

"You keep saying that, Jack, but where's my girl?" Emmy's dad yelled. "I can't just sit at home and wait to receive her fingers in the mail. I demand action. I want her back, now!"

"What is your response to these poor parents?" the reporter said.

Jack stopped and looked at her. I could tell he was about to say something I feared he was going to regret later on, so I grabbed his arm and pulled him away from her and through the crowd.

"Don't say another word," I said. "They'll only use it against you."

CHAPTER THIRTY-SIX
May 2018

"**S**he hasn't come back. What do you think happened to her?"

A couple of girls were talking behind Alicia as she sat on the mattress and stared at the metal plate above them where Alondra had disappeared the day before. It had been a long night inside the box truck. Barely any of them had said a word. All they could hear all night was the sound of Emmy throwing up.

"You think they sent her home?" The girl named Trudy asked. Her voice had a little ray of hope in it, but it didn't last long.

Alicia didn't know her well but knew she was in fourth grade, one grade level below her. Alicia didn't like to think about what had happened to Alondra, who used to be her best friend, but still, she couldn't stop. Was it really possible that they sent her home?

"Of course, they didn't send her home," the girl named Britney said. She was also a fourth grader, and Alicia believed she was in the same class as Trudy but wasn't sure.

"Th-then what did they do to her?" Trudy asked, her voice wavering in uncertainty.

No one knew the answer to that nor did anyone even try and bring a comforting one. Alicia feared the worst and she guessed so did the rest of them. She felt like crying when thinking about it, so she tried not to, but it was hard, almost impossible not to imagine what had happened to her. Alicia felt bad. She loved Alondra and missed her so much. Every day, she had hoped that Alondra would stop hanging out with Tonya and return to be with Alicia again like they used to be. Was it too late now?

It can't be. There's so much we haven't done together. We were going to make slime together, remember? We were going to do it in my yard since your mom wouldn't have it anywhere near her house. My mom had finally caved in and said yes if it stayed outside. That was all before you left me for Tonya, and we never got to it, remember?

Alicia sniffled and wiped a tear away from her cheek. All night long, she had waited and sort of expected to see Alondra come back. Maybe they would have beaten her, maybe even badly, but at least she was…still…at least she was still…

"They killed her, didn't they?" Trudy then said, her lower lip shuddering as she said the words.

A shiver of fear rushed through the burning hot box truck.

"Hey, we don't know that," Julie yelled. She was still caring for Nikki, who didn't seem to be getting any better. "For all we know, they sent her home, okay?"

No one agreed with her because no one believed it. They had all looked into the barrels of those guns; they had all pleaded for their lives and seen how they looked at them when they asked to go to the restroom. They saw it in their eyes behind those nasty skin-colored pantyhose that distorted their faces.

They didn't care.

CHAPTER THIRTY-SEVEN

June 1999

B arely out of the hospital, Jane found herself in a shelter for women. She had no money and nowhere else to go. The people at the shelter gave her a room with a small kitchen so she could take care of herself and the children. Jane couldn't remember ever being more relieved than she was at the moment she closed the door and sat down on the couch. No more walking on eggshells; no more fearing what mood he was in when he came home; no more terrified hours wondering what he was going to do next. Now, it was just her and the kids.

It was all she needed.

Within days of arriving at the shelter, Jane had a visitor. A lady who presented herself as Colleen West, a caseworker with the Children's Protection Services came to her door and knocked. She let her inside, and they sat down on the small hard couch that came with the room.

Colleen was a small woman with glasses and wore a grey cardigan over her pink turtleneck. She looked more like a librarian to Jane with her hair in a bun and everything, but she seemed nice and had a friendly smile, so when she asked Jane to tell her the entire story, she did. She told her about Bob and how he had grown worse over the years, and how she had to get away from him in the end. She even told her how he had hit poor Anna, but Colleen had already heard that from the hospital.

"And you were pretty badly beaten as well, I heard," she said and placed a hand on top of Jane's.

Jane cried and nodded, letting her emotions out for the first time in a very long time, and for the first time, she felt like someone actually wanted to listen. Colleen seemed actually to care.

"It must have been very rough for all of you. You did the right thing in leaving him."

Jane sighed, relieved, and wiped her eyes with a tissue that Colleen handed her. She was so filled with guilt and doubt since he was, after all, the father of her children.

"On the good days, when he was in a good mood, we actually had a great marriage," she said for some reason, maybe to justify her choice not to have left him earlier. "It was just those…other days and you never knew when they would hit. He would come home from work and be all over me because I had made something for dinner he didn't care for, or if he thought I had been on the phone with my friend Annabelle. He kept track of the calls made from the phone in our house. I couldn't even call my mother. He would tell me I had changed and that something was different about me when I had. He believed my mother was trying to get me to leave him, that she somehow had this power over me to make me do stuff like that…but the reality was that I wanted to leave him, I just didn't know how to."

"Maybe he sensed that's what you wanted and that was actually what he feared the most," she said, then looked around and spotted the kids. Three of them, Vanessa, Penelope, and Elisa were all playing quietly, while Matthew was sleeping in a chair. Only Anna wasn't doing anything. She was sitting by the window, staring out of it, not saying a word or even playing.

"Mind if I talk to her for a little?" Colleen asked.

Jane shook her head. "Of course not. She's been struggling since it happened."

Colleen sent her another sympathetic smile before approaching the girl. "It's only natural."

CHAPTER THIRTY-EIGHT

May 2018

Jack showed me to his desk, then asked if I wanted coffee and left. I sat down in a chair and looked at the pictures of his family in the middle of all his mess. Between him and Shannon, they had a lot of children. She was a famous country singer but, coming from Denmark, I didn't know much about country music, so I had no idea who she was before I met her.

"So, how's the family?" I asked as he returned with my coffee. "How's your daughter?"

Jack sighed and sat down. He rubbed his head, then shook it. "Not well. She's still struggling."

I knew his adoptive daughter, Emily, struggled with anorexia and had been admitted to a place that knew how to deal with it, but once she got out, she continued starving herself. She had just gotten better at hiding it from them. Shannon had told me about it once when we had them all over for dinner.

"I'm sorry to hear that," I said, sending him a compassionate smile. "I hope she'll get better soon."

"Yeah, well, you and me both. It's a process, though."

I sipped my coffee, the nagging sensation of worry growing

inside me as I thought about my own daughter. It was hard to remain calm with what I had seen this morning.

Jack asked me to repeat everything I had told him earlier, and he wrote it all down while I spoke. I was in the middle of a sentence when I heard someone yell from the interrogation rooms. I looked up and into Jack's eyes.

He shook his head. "He's not exactly cooperating."

"Mr. Meckler?"

Jack drank from his cup that read WORLD'S BEST FARTER on the side of it. Putting it down, he nodded. There was more yelling, and I recognized Mr. Meckler's voice.

"I've told you a million times. I don't know anything. I don't know where those kids are! Please, just let me go. PLEASE!"

I stared in the direction of the sound and started to bite my nails. I felt such deep anger and resentment rising inside of me thinking that, in there, only a few yards from me sat the man who might have my kid, who might know where she was. The guy had to be somehow involved in all this, right? I felt convinced he was. Why couldn't he just break down and tell us everything?

I turned my head back and looked at Jack, who seemed to be lost in his thoughts as well.

"How are we on the kids who were also waiting for the bus? What are they saying?" I asked.

Jack scoffed. "Nothing so far. Some remember Mr. Meckler talking to some of the girls, while others say they saw Mrs. Baker talking to them."

"What about that tip?" I then asked.

"What tip?"

"Yesterday when I talked to you on the phone, someone came up to you and told you there was a tip you needed to look at."

"Ah, that." He shook his head and drank more coffee. "That was nothing."

"It must have been something if you rushed to check it out, right?"

Jack took in a deep breath and looked at me, scrutinizing me.

"You really don't give up, do you. Mrs. Franck? Is that the reporter in you?"

"Maybe. Or the mother who desperately wants answers."

He nodded. "Fair enough. I guess there's no harm in telling you. It was a tip from someone telling us about some strange activity out at the quarry inland, a place called White Rock. But we went there, and there was nothing."

"What kind of strange activity?" I asked.

"People hanging out there. Cars. A guy who walked his dog nearby every day told us there was never usually anyone there, but lately, he had seen people there. My guess is that he witnessed a drug deal go down, but that's not what we're investigating right now. We went there, and there was nothing to see. It was a dead end. No trace of our girls."

Once Jack was done taking my statement, I said goodbye to him with a hug, and once again he promised me he was going to find Julie alive, but this time I found that I felt it harder to believe him. As I walked down the hallway toward the exit, the door to the inter-rogation room opened up, and two officers were leading out Mr. Meckler. I held my breath as he walked past, the eyes of a raving madman glaring down at me.

CHAPTER THIRTY-NINE

May 2018

They had set up a Crisis Psychologist and Family Support Center at the parking lot next to Juice N' Java. I went to get myself a sandwich for lunch but ended up talking to a lot of the other parents who had sought out help there. A woman who spoke with a very calm voice approached me and asked me if I needed to talk.

"I'm good," I said. It wasn't that I didn't want to talk; it was more because I knew that once I opened up, I was afraid I wouldn't be able to shut it off again.

A guy was sitting in a chair, and they were taking his blood pressure. He pushed a woman away, yelling at her:

"I don't need you to check my darn blood pressure. I just need my daughter back!"

The tension was visible on all the faces and I thought that maybe it would be better if everyone just went home. But then again, I realized I didn't even want to go home. I couldn't stand the thought of sitting there waiting for my phone to ring. And I certainly didn't want to go home and empty the mailbox and find my daughter's fingers in some creepy letter.

That was when I spotted Mrs. Baker. She was sitting in a chair, talking to one of the parents, comforting her, talking and smiling, putting a hand on the poor mother's arm. The mother thanked her with a long hug, then left.

"Mrs. Baker," I said and approached her, leaning on my crutch.

"Rebekka," she said and got up. She gave me a warm motherly hug. She looked me in the eyes. "How are you holding up, you poor thing?"

"I…well not too good, I have to admit."

Mrs. Baker shook her head. "It's is incomprehensible. All of it. Those poor girls and now with that…*letter*." She whispered the last word like it was a curse word.

"I know. I was there when Nancy got it," I said and sat down next to Mrs. Baker.

"That must have been awful, sweetheart. I am so sorry. I can only imagine how all of you must be feeling. I've known the kids for years and treated them all for scraped knees or checked them for lice over the years. I feel terrible. I can't believe he would have done such a thing."

"You mean Mr. Meckler?" I asked.

She nodded. "I didn't know that bus wasn't supposed to be there. How could I? Our job was to get the kids on the buses, and that's what we did. How could I have known what he was up to?"

She gave me a sad look. "I just can't believe that nice man could have taken all those girls. And then sending a letter with the girl's… fingers in it and that rhyme. What is that even supposed to mean? *Ten Little Injuns*?"

My eyes met hers as she said the words, and something struck inside me. The choice of the nursery rhyme couldn't be just a random thing, could it? Did it mean something? Was it a message from the kidnapper?

"It's a riddle," I said.

"What's that, sweetheart?"

"The rest of the verse is missing. It's a riddle," I repeated, then got up with my phone in my hand. As I thanked Mrs. Baker, I walked away, Googling the lyrics to *Ten Little Injuns* with the one hand that wasn't holding a crutch.

CHAPTER FORTY

June 1999

A t first, she thought the knock on her door was part of her
dream, but as it grew louder and harder, Jane realized there
was actually someone at her door. She blinked and looked at her
watch.

"Who knocks on someone's door at two a.m.?"

Jane was still at the shelter, so she assumed it had to be one of
the other residents and not someone from the outside. It couldn't be
Bob, could it? She opened the door.

"Colleen?"

Colleen wasn't alone. She had two police officers with her and a
note in her hand that she showed Jane.

"This is not a social call. This is an inspection," she said. "I will
let you know that you're being investigated for abuse and neglect."

Thinking she had to be still dreaming or at least hearing Colleen
wrong, Jane stared at the woman, baffled.

"Excuse me, what?"

Colleen walked straight into the kitchen and looked into the
fridge. After that, she went through all the cabinets and stopped at
the dirty dishes in the sink. Then she wrote something on her
notepad.

"Colleen? I don't understand...what is...?"

"Where are the children?" Colleen asked, approaching her again.

"Well, they're sleeping, of course."

"Then wake them up."

"Wake them up? Why? I don't understand? Colleen, what's going on? Can you please tell me what's happening?"

"I need to check them for bruises and marks. Please have them get out of bed," she said, her voice as cold as steel.

"No," Jane said. "I don't want to wake up my kids in the middle of the night. It's hard enough for them to sleep as it is after all they've been through. You can check them in the morning if it's that important."

Colleen turned on her heel and stared at Jane. "You're making me nervous here. It is my responsibility to make sure these kids are safe. It is my job, and I take it very seriously. If I miss even a small trace that could have told me your kids are being abused, then it will be my responsibility if they end up in the hospital or...dead."

"My kids aren't being abused," Jane said. "I was."

"And Anna," Colleen said.

"Yes, by her dad, but we moved away from him, remember? We left."

Colleen wasn't listening; she was checking the floors for dirt, then taking notes.

"If you don't get the children out here for me to look at, then these officers will take them away from you. Is that what you want?" Colleen said.

Jane felt like crying. What the heck was this? Why was Colleen suddenly being like this? She had been so nice the other day and now this? Now she was talking about taking Jane's kids?

Jane nodded then walked to the bedroom where the kids slept on mattresses on the floor. She walked inside and woke them up one after another and had them come out to Colleen, who asked them to take off their clothes. She then checked each and every one of them, even little Matthew, who was still very much asleep in Jane's arms as she did it.

Then Colleen walked into the bedroom and looked at the children's beds. "What is he sleeping in?" she said and pointed at Matthew.

"He sleeps with his sister. On a mattress."

"That doesn't sound very safe. You don't have a crib?"

"No. I had nothing when I came here. You know this, Colleen, why are you acting this way?"

Colleen wrote on her pad, then looked up at Jane. "I only have the children's best interest in mind, that's all. It's all about the children."

CHAPTER FORTY-ONE

May 2018

"I think it's a riddle," I repeated when coming home to Sune. I had taken an Uber back while looking through the lyrics to the song on my phone. Sune was sitting in the living room with William, doing a huge puzzle. He had decided to skip his physical training today after what had happened at Nancy's house and me having to go downtown to the police station.

They had already finished half of the tiger's face. I had kept Sune updated, so he knew what was going on, yet he still didn't quite understand what I was talking about.

"What's a riddle?"

"The song. In the letter. Remember how I told you about it?"

Sune looked down at William, then told him that *Daddy had to go talk to Mommy for a little.* We went out on the porch and closed the sliding door behind us.

"Okay, now you can tell me," Sune said. "I just didn't want William to…you know."

"Oh, no, me either," I said. "He's getting so smart. He understands so much now."

We sat on the patio couch and looked out over the ocean. I

couldn't really enjoy it, though, since so many thoughts were rambling through my mind in what felt like a constant rotation.

"I think the kidnappers are trying to tell us something," I said, "by using the line from the nursery rhyme."

"Okay, that sounds plausible, but exactly what are they telling us?"

"Ten Little Injuns, right? There are ten girls. So, the first one goes like this:

Ten little Injuns standin' in a line,
One toddled home
And then there were nine."

Sune looked at me, confused. "So, what are you saying? That Alondra *toddled home*? What does that even mean?"

I took in a deep breath. "I don't know. I keep searching for some deeper meaning to it, but I can't seem to find it."

A flock of pelicans floated past us, looking like their lives required no effort whatsoever. That's when I thought of something.

"What if there is none?" I asked.

"What do you mean?"

I leaned forward. "What if it is exactly what it says?"

"You mean she actually toddled home?" Sune stared at me in disbelief. "You mean she is at home? I don't understand…"

I rose to my feet, still leaning on the crutch. My leg was hurting, but I had no time to feel sorry for myself.

"What do you mean, Rebekka? Rebekka?" he said, confused. "Where are you going?"

I hurried the best I could to the door, then opened it. "If I'm right, then I'm going to find Alondra."

CHAPTER FORTY-TWO

May 2018

I almost ran to the sidewalk toward Nancy's house. I completely ignored the pain in my leg as I approached her house and the place where I had been sitting with her just a few hours earlier when her world had come crashing down.

My heart was in my throat as I wondered if they would even believe me.

It was, of course, her husband, Kyle, who opened the door.

"Rebekka?"

I took in a deep breath. "I know it's a bad time for you and Nancy, but can I come in?"

He looked dumbfounded. "Listen, Rebekka. We've been through a lot...Nancy is..."

"It's important," I said. "Very important."

I could tell he was about to deny me entrance when something made him change his mind. Maybe it was the look in my eyes, maybe the tone of my voice. He could tell I was being sincere.

He nodded. "Sure." He stepped aside so I could walk in. "Nancy is still out, though. If you were planning on talking to her."

"I wasn't," I said and walked into the living room while Kyle closed the door behind me.

I stood still for a few seconds, listening, as he came up behind me. "You care to tell me what's going on?"

"Have you heard any noises today, any unusual sounds?" I asked.

He looked like he thought I was an idiot, which he probably did, but I didn't care at this point.

"I…I haven't thought about it, no."

"No knocking or hammering or…say…what's that smell?" I asked.

"Rebekka…I have…it's been a long…we're exhausted and just want to…" he sniffed the air. "That *is* strange. I noticed it earlier too when I was in the kitchen but didn't think anything of it. Now, I smell it again."

I walked toward a door where the smell was worse. Fumes were coming from underneath it. Invisible fumes were slowly seeping into the living room.

My heart stopped.

"What is it?" Kyle asked.

"Go get Nancy, now!"

"But…"

"Kyle, I'm serious. You need to get out of here, both of you, now!"

He rushed to get her while I walked to the front door and opened it. I walked outside and toward the garage. Fumes were oozing from underneath the garage door as well.

I called Jack as I spotted Kyle carrying Nancy outside. I signaled for him to keep going. To get as far away from the house as possible.

"Now what, Rebekka?" Jack asked.

"You need to come."

He sighed. "Really? This better be good. I'm busy."

I ignored his remark. The fumes were reaching my nostrils, and I backed up.

"Just come, will you? And bring an ambulance and the fire-fighters as well."

CHAPTER FORTY-THREE

May 2018

They arrived less than three minutes later. One of the advantages of living in a small town, I guess. The police station and fire department were just down the road from us.

I stood with Kyle and Nancy—who had woken up—and their son J.T. on the sidewalk while the firefighters drove up in their big trucks, then swarmed the driveway. Nancy threw up on the pavement, then complained about not feeling well.

"It's like something's wrong with my heart, Kyle," she wailed and bent over, clinging to her husband. "It's beating funny, Kyle. It's beating funny! Why is it doing that?"

Dressed in full gear, the firefighters opened the garage door where Nancy's car was parked.

It was still running.

"Someone's in there," one of them yelled when he looked inside it.

My heart stopped. This was exactly what I had feared.

Kyle didn't look too well either and, seconds later, he too bent over and threw up, then held his hands to his head while the firefighters leaned inside the open window of the car and desperately tried to pull the person out. I could hear them yelling at one another that *she was strapped down.*

"Bring something to cut her loose."

A second later, they pulled out a small body and rushed her out into the driveway. An arm poked out. It was missing two fingers.

"Alondra!" Nancy said, then tried to run to her, but Kyle held her back forcefully. Almost without breathing, I watched as they performed CPR on the girl, then pulled out the defibrillator and used that on her, but after several desperate attempts had to give up.

All eyes turned to look at Nancy and Kyle.

"NOOOOO!"

Nancy screamed, finally getting loose from Kyle's grip—or maybe he let her go since he too realized it was over. Nancy ran to her daughter, letting out a weeping scream that went straight through every bone in my body. Kyle sunk to his knees and threw up again, while Nancy took her daughter frantically in her arms. The firefighters pulled away and took off their helmets in respect, while Nancy screamed and carried her daughter around, not knowing where to go or why she was even doing it, just screaming and crying loudly, letting her pain out.

Finally, she turned toward her husband.

"She was in there all this time, Kyle. She was in there, in our own home and we didn't...we didn't know, Kyle. We didn't. We could have saved her, Kyle. We could have saved her!"

Saying this, Nancy sunk to her knees, sobbing. She held her daughter tightly to her chest, rocking her back and forth, her cries in such deep a despair it made me want to scream.

"We need to get you all to the hospital," a firefighter said and placed a compassionate hand on her shoulder. "You have all been exposed to the carbon monoxide."

Like it was their cue in some cruel horror show, the paramedics from the ambulance rushed to her and separated her from her dead daughter, then put her on a stretcher and rolled her away, while Nancy was still yelling her daughter's name.

CHAPTER FORTY-FOUR

May 2018

Julie breathed raggedly. There was very little oxygen left inside the box truck and, along with the excruciating heat, it had made them all sleepy. Several of the girls had dozed off and hadn't woken up at all during the day. Julie grabbed a package of cereal and started to eat from it, then flushed the dry mass down with water. Many of the other girls had stopped eating, and she couldn't blame them at this point. The stench inside the coffin made it hard to muster any type of appetite, and they had begun asking themselves, *what did it matter anyway?*

Julie still had hope. How she kept it was a mystery. But she had it. She wasn't going to give up anytime soon. She would rather die fighting for her life. But that was just her. That was who she was.

She crunched another handful of cheerios and looked at Nikki in the corner. Her fever was constant. It was neither going up nor down, but she had hardly been awake at all the past two days, and it worried Julie.

She looked up at the hatch above them, where Alondra had disappeared. She kept wondering if she would come back from there. She tried not to, but she couldn't stop thinking about her and what they had done to her. She liked to imagine that she had been sent home. That maybe the kidnappers had asked for a ransom, and as soon as they got the money, they let her go. She liked that thought, that Alondra was back with her parents, playing on the beach or at least hugging her mother again and not stuck here in this stinky underground tomb.

Because if it could happen to her, then it might happen to the rest of them too. They would get to go home. It was still possible. It had to be.

Alicia came up next to Julie and sat down with a deep sigh. Julie handed her the box of cereal. Alicia shook her head.

"You should eat," Julie said. "You haven't had anything all day."

They had thrown more boxes of cereal down when taking Alondra out. Some of them had spilled all over the floor. The girls had screamed in panic when they closed the hatch again, and darkness had once again surrounded them. There was a small lamp in the corner under the ceiling, but it wasn't lighting up the entire box truck, and it was getting weaker by the day. It had gone out a few times, then come back on, with the result that the girls screamed in panic till it returned. Julie dreaded the day it would turn out completely. What would happen then? Would they just leave them there in complete darkness? Julie prepared herself for it to happen and, every day, she memorized where everything was. Where the toilet boxes were and where the food and water were. She even practiced finding it all closing her eyes, so she would be able to get by in complete darkness.

Yet the thought terrified her.

Alicia grabbed the cereal box and took a handful of cheerios and ate them, crunching loudly. Julie smiled, relieved. Those that ate were the ones who would survive the longest. And Julie wanted Alicia to stay with her. She wanted Nikki to also, but she wasn't sure she would. Julie had given up on getting her to eat and knew that she didn't have long anymore.

The thought was tormenting.

Julie glanced up toward the hatch once again, thinking about Alondra and sunlight and fresh air, when there was a noise above them, and the hatch was opened. Julie stood up and took in a couple of deep breaths. The few girls that were still awake rushed to the place beneath the hatch and started to scream.

Another pantyhose-covered face peeked down at them.

"Please," Julie said. "There are sick children down here. Please, let us out or at least take the sick ones out, please, sir."

She pleaded, but the man didn't listen. He sunk the ladder down and started to descend. Halfway down, the ladder was surrounded by the girls, trying to grab onto it, but seeing the rifle swung over his shoulder, they backed up. The man looked around, then pointed at Emmy.

"Her. Yes, you. Come here. You're next."

CHAPTER FORTY-FIVE

May 2018

"You saved their lives."

Jack had brought me a bouquet of flowers. He was standing in the doorway holding them out to me.

"This is from all of us in the fire and police department. We thought you would like a little token of appreciation for your heroic action."

I grabbed the flowers, then started to cry again. I had been crying all night and morning. I couldn't un-see the images of Nancy holding her dead daughter in her arms, and they kept haunting me.

"I really don't think there was anything heroic…"

"Can I come in?" Jack asked.

I sighed. "Why not? You want some coffee?"

"That would be perfect, thanks."

We went to the kitchen where William was playing on his iPad. Sune was at his physical training, and Tobias was playing some game on his computer. It had been a very quiet morning except for my crying.

I put the flowers in water and handed Jack a cup of coffee. I wasn't using the crutch today, but still holding onto things when needed. I was still in pain, but it wasn't too bad anymore.

"I really don't feel like I deserve them," I said and placed the flowers on our breakfast counter.

"Are you kidding me?" Jack said. "If it weren't for you, the entire family would have ended up getting killed. Carbon Monoxide is no joke. That car had been running for at least six hours, they say. The fumes were seeping into the house. Nancy and Kyle owe you their lives. Not to mention their son's."

I sat down heavily. "That may be, but had I come sooner, then I could have saved the girl too. If I had come earlier, if only I had figured the riddle out earlier. I keep thinking about it, that even an hour earlier might have made a huge difference."

"It's very easy to think that way, but you have to stop it. In my line of work, there is always a *what if*, but I can't let myself think that way. What happened happened; there is nothing you can do to change it."

"So basically, you just have to become a cold bastard," I said with an exhausted scoff. He wasn't exactly making me feel better about myself. I wasn't someone who could just turn that sort of thing off.

"If that's what it takes, then yes."

I sipped my coffee. It tasted horrible, but then again, everything seemed to taste like that stench I had smelled inside of Nancy's house. I hadn't been able to get anything down ever since. It all tasted like that smell.

The stench of death sneaking up on you.

"So, the kidnappers placed her in the car and strapped her down for us to find?" I asked. "Why would they do that?"

Jack shrugged. "Beats me. We still haven't received any demands from them. It's certainly not textbook. We have, however, arrested Mr. Meckler. We're charging him with accessory to kidnapping. We think we have enough."

I nodded and sipped more coffee. "That sounds good. Still doesn't give us our kids back, though, does it?"

"Hopefully, the search of his house will lead to something. We're getting information about all of his whereabouts over the past several months, you know, from credit cards and phone companies and access to his phone and computers. It is my hope that this will bring us closer to where they are keeping your kids."

"Let's hope so," I said with a deep exhale. "Let's hope so."

CHAPTER FORTY-SIX

June 1999

In family court, Jane sat still, mouth gaping as she listened to Colleen telling the judge why she believed Jane wasn't fit to take proper care of her own children.

"She has no job; she has no way of providing for them," she said. "Feeding five children is a big expense. It is a lot of work. It's not easy to do on your own. On several occasions during my visits, her home has been observed to be highly unsanitary. The fridge was almost empty. Jane just came out of a very abusive relationship, one that left her daughter, Anna, hurt and Jane hospitalized. She couldn't manage to protect the child from her father's rage, even though she was in the same room when it happened. My conclusion is that she is simply emotionally exhausted; she is terribly trauma-tized and needs professional help. Having five children to attend to is not good for someone in her state."

Someone in my state? What is that supposed to mean? I am not in any state. I am here and feel better than ever.

But Jane wasn't allowed to say anything. All she could do was sit there and listen to Colleen's arguments and accusations, most of which she found to be extremely insulting.

"Furthermore, she refused to participate in drug treatment

despite admitting that she smoked marijuana—and I quote, your honor— "whenever I get the urge," and she has missed two child-safety conferences provided to her by the shelter, and therefore I believe she poses an imminent risk to the children's lives and health."

I was talking about when I was younger. Not now. I don't smoke anything now. She's twisting my words. Why is she allowed just to stand there and speak about me like that and I can't do anything about it?

Jane felt like screaming and yelling it out, but Iris from the shelter had told her to keep her temper down. Any outburst on her part would be considered hostile and would be used against her. So, she bit her lip and kept quiet while Colleen continued.

"One of the children suffers from eczema, another is under-weight, and Anna, whom we mentioned earlier, the one who was beaten by her father, is getting more and more closed off every time I see her. I fear for her emotional state, and I fear that Jane Wilson simply is failing to provide proper care for them. She's not a bad mother; it's just too much for her. I recommend that the children be placed with their aunt and uncle until their mother has found a suit-able place to live, found a job to provide for them, agreed to take parenting classes, and submits herself to inspections by our case-workers and works with us willingly."

"You're kidding me, right?" Jane said out loud, rising to her feet in anger. "You can't do that. You can't take my kids!"

But she could. And she did. The judge agreed with Colleen and, on that same day, Bob's brother Jim and his wife Melissa walked away with all five of Jane's children.

CHAPTER FORTY-SEVEN

May 2018

There were footsteps above their heads. Julie and Alicia looked at one another, then back up at the hatch. The kidnappers usually didn't come at this time of day. They came at night when it was dark out.

"Someone's here," Julie said.

"Is it Alondra coming back?" Tonya asked hopefully.

"Or Emmy?" Haley asked.

Julie didn't know if she actually hoped it was them. She wanted them to be back at home instead, so probably not. But she would still love to see them alive, to know that they hadn't been harmed.

"Let's just wait and see," Julie said.

The footsteps above them paused, and for a while, it was very quiet.

"What if it isn't them?" Haley asked.

"What do you mean?" Julie said wiping sweat from her face with her arm. She couldn't remember how long it had been since she last showered. It felt like even the dirt on her body had dirt on it. She had kept track of the days by ripping a part of a cereal box off but, even so, she was slowly beginning to lose track of how long they had been underground. They all were. It was easy since there was no sunlight. The few of them that wore watches had them taken away along with their phones. It was probably because the kidnappers were scared someone would be wearing an Apple watch and would use it to call for help, or maybe it could be traced, Julie figured.

"What if it isn't the kidnappers? What if it's someone else?" Haley continued, a sudden ray of hope in her voice.

"Yeah, what if it's the police?" Tonya said. "What if they've come to look for us?"

The girls glanced at one another, hope springing to their eyes.

"We have to tell them where we are," Haley said.

"We should yell," Tonya said, then rose to her feet. She walked to the area beneath the hatch, then yelled.

"HELP!"

Haley soon joined Tonya, then Alicia did the same, and, seconds later, Trudy and Britney woke up and started to yell too.

"HEEELP! WE'RE DOWN HERE!"

Thinking it could do them no harm, it wasn't like their situation could get any worse, Julie soon chimed in. She screamed at the top of her lungs, then turned to glance at the other girls, who, for the first time in days, seemed hopeful. They screamed and yelled and banged on the sides of the box truck, trying to make a noise. Then they heard something. The sound of a voice yelling from above them. The sound was subdued and felt very far away; still, they had no doubt they heard it.

"HELLO?"

The sound made all the girls go silent for a second before they burst into laughter and even louder screams.

"We're down here, help us, please!"

CHAPTER FORTY-EIGHT

May 2018

I had to check. I knew Jack had already been there with all his officers and searched it, but I had to see for myself. So, after Jack had left, I waited for a little while till Sune came back from his training. The woman, the physical therapist, who was working with him, picked him up and brought him back every day now, so he didn't really need my help anymore. I then drove to White Rock Quarry. I parked the car in the gravel and got out. The place seemed very empty. There were two cranes and what looked like bulldozers and crawler tractors. In the distance, there were several wheel loaders used to transport the rocks. But that was pretty much it. Except for a small shack I spotted now when looking to my right. It looked like it would blow away at any time a hurricane dropped by. It was a mystery how it was still standing.

I decided to walk to it and knock on the door. No one opened the door, and so I knocked again, but still, nothing happened. I looked in the window and saw what looked like a small office and a lunchroom, probably for the workers. But no one seemed to be working at the quarry, and I wondered if it had been empty for a long time.

I decided to take a little walk around the site. My toes in my flip-flops soon turned white from the dust. I was beginning to sweat heavily in the burning sun and drank some water from the bottle I had brought. I stopped and looked around. As I drank my water, I was certain I heard something, but I wasn't sure. The sand beneath my feet looked different than everywhere else, almost like someone had dug there recently. I touched it with my foot but only found more sand beneath.

"Hello?" I said, then yelled till I heard the echo bounce off the walls surrounding me.

"HELLO?"

All I could hear was my own voice repeating the word. I then continued walking forward. My foot kicked something, and I looked down at a strange sight.

That's odd? An empty cereal box? Guess you can find trash anywhere these days.

I bent down and picked it up, then looked around for a trash can but couldn't find any. It wasn't a place that was meant for people to be taking a stroll, so I decided to go back to the car instead before I got myself in trouble.

I threw the empty cereal box in the back, then took one more glance around the quarry. There really wasn't anywhere you could hide ten girls, I concluded, then got back inside the car and took off.

CHAPTER FORTY-NINE

May 2018

"Hello? We're down here!"

Julie yelled as loud as she could. The girls continued banging on the sides till their hands burned. They were yelling and screaming, but still, nothing happened.

There was movement again on top of them. More footsteps. But they suddenly sounded like they were going away.

NO!

"Don't leave! Come back! We're down here! We're right down here! Help us; please, help us. Hello? HELLO?"

Julie yelled at the top of her lungs, then hammered her hands on the sides again and again as hard as she could, while yelling and screaming. Her hands were red and throbbing in pain.

Still, nothing happened.

"Whoever it was, they're gone," Haley said. She turned away from Julie and walked to a mattress, where she sat down with a deep exhale. Tonya joined her shortly after.

"No!" Julie yelled, refusing to give up. "It can't be. It can't. The world is not that cruel. Come back! COME BACK!"

Julie wasn't going to stop. Someone was up there; someone had found the place and that someone was looking for them. She just knew they were. They had to be. They simply had to be. And if only they made enough noise, that someone would come back, they would hear them and come back.

Forcedly denying the harsh reality that was slowly creeping up on her, Julie continued banging and yelling even long after the other girls had stopped. Then, when she finally ran out of breath and strength, she fell to her knees, hiding her face between her hands. With every tear she cried in the minutes after that, the hope that she had clung to so tightly slowly faded out and left.

CHAPTER FIFTY

May 2018

I rolled the window down as I drove back toward the barrier islands and Cocoa Beach. I wanted to feel the wind on my face, but it was so warm, I soon had enough and rolled the window back up and cranked up the AC. I wondered if Julie was somewhere she could feel that warm wind too. That was her favorite part about Florida. That she was never cold. Even on cloudy or rainy days. Back in Denmark, she always wore extra clothes, like stockings beneath her jeans in order to keep warm enough, and yet she would still freeze. I wondered if she was keeping warm where she was. Was she getting enough to eat and drink? Were they beating her?

I shook the thought. I couldn't let myself think about it. I couldn't go down that path. I admitted I hadn't expected to find much at the quarry, but there was a small part of me that had allowed myself to hope, just a little bit, that I would find my daughter there. But I knew it was a long shot since Jack and his colleagues had already been there and checked it out when they received the tip.

Probably just a drug deal.

I drove past the bridges and back onto the island, then passed our house and went to Juice N' Java. There, I met a group of other parents sitting outside. This was what I needed right now. Usually, I would love to hang out with Sune and talk to him about what I was going through, but somehow, I got the feeling that he didn't really understand. Besides, he had so much else to deal with right now. I wanted him to focus on getting better and doing his training, and he was always so exhausted when he came home from his therapy, I figured the last thing he wanted was to listen to me and all my fears and anxieties.

No, I needed to talk to people who understood me and who were going through the same thing I was, so I parked the car and walked to the group, grabbed a chair, and sat down. Emmy's dad, John, handed me a cup of coffee and I took it with a smile.

"Just what I needed."

Mary and Sue were there too, and a couple, Jennifer and Toby that I had gotten to know as Nikki's parents. Nikki was the youngest of the children that had been kidnapped.

There was a silence between us all, but that didn't matter. It felt good—or at least less painful—to sit there with people who were going through the same thing as I was. I didn't have to hold back; I didn't have to explain anything. I could just be.

"Anyone talked to Nancy and Kyle today?" John asked.

They all shook their heads and looked down at their feet or at the coffee cups in their hands. I spotted the owner of Juice N' Java as she was putting out more sandwiches. The search teams weren't as big as they used to be, but there were still some brave men and women out there looking for our children in every dune of the beach, knocking on doors of houses, and checking every creek and canal or even people's backyards. There were people in boats sailing around the canals looking for them, and that made me feel good. Only I wasn't so sure our kids were in Cocoa Beach anymore. I knew the police had search teams out in the area where the bus was found too, but it was such a vast area that there really wasn't much to search except the swamps and they were doing that too, but who would hide children in a swamp?

None of us dared to speak about Nancy and Kyle or what happened to them. It was still too painful to think about. Up until we found Alondra, I guess we had all still hoped we would get our kids home alive. Now the hope was dwindling fast.

"They're still in the hospital last I heard," I said and sipped my coffee.

"Will they be okay?" Mary asked with a slight sniffle.

I cleared my throat. "As far as I heard, yes. They suffered a poisoning but made it out in time."

"I couldn't…I mean, I can't even imagine…" Mary said.

"I don't want to imagine," John said. "I don't even want to think about it. Any part of it."

"Such a tragedy," Sue said, her voice shivering.

And then we all went quiet again, looking down and not at one another. I sipped my coffee. John looked up at the sky.

"They say it might rain later."

For some reason, that made the rest of us look up at the sky too, and when our eyes met across the table, something had changed. Here was something normal we could talk about and I guess it was all we longed for at this point. Normalcy.

"Really?" Mary said. "It doesn't look much like rain to me."

"You know how it is at this time of year," Sue said. "It pops up out of nowhere. Gotta watch out for those pop-up storms."

"True. Gotta love Florida, right? And they say we don't have seasons. The way I see it, there are four seasons. Love-bug-season, Hurricane-season, tourist-season, and summer."

And just like that, the mood was heightened in the group. It felt so relieving to talk about something ordinary.

John rose to his feet. "Anyone want more coffee? I noticed they just brought out a new pot."

We all nodded, and he took our cups one by one and filled them. I asked for a little milk in mine. Mary sent me half a smile.

"You know what Julie said to my daughter the other day?"

"No?"

"She told her she was pretty. It meant so much to her, she came home and told me. You know how insecure they are at this age."

"Wow," I said, sending her my own version of half a smile. "I'm glad to hear that. Really glad."

"I thought you might be happy to hear it. You have a great daughter. Very compassionate toward others. My daughter says that if you ever need a shoulder to cry on, you can be sure to find one on Julie."

"Thank you for telling me that," I said as John handed me back my cup with a gentle hand on my shoulder. I thanked him as he took Sue's cup. On his way back to the coffee pot to re-fill it, he stopped when his phone vibrated in his pants. He put down the cup and pulled it out. I knew something was terribly wrong when I noticed that his hand holding the phone began to shake violently.

CHAPTER FIFTY-ONE

May 2018

"What's wrong? John?"
I rushed to my feet so fast that I knocked over my coffee and it spilled everywhere.

"John?"

He barely moved except for the shaking, while he stared at the display on his phone.

"John?"

He looked up, and his glare met mine. The look in his eyes made my heart beat faster. He turned the phone, so I could see what he was looking at. It was a text from an unknown number.

"What's going on?" Mary said with a light shriek to her voice. "What's happening?"

"It's a text," I said and faced them. "A text with the next verse."

"The next verse? I don't under...what does it say?" Sue asked, rising to her feet.

"*Nine little Injuns swingin' on a gate,*" I read out loud.

"W-what...what does that mean?" Mary asked.

"Yeah, what does it mean?" Toby said.

"The other one, the letter that Nancy and Kyle received...that was the same, right? That was the first verse, right?" his wife Jennifer asked.

"Yes," I said.

"And that was a riddle, right?" Mary said.

I nodded.

"So, this must be another riddle, right?" Mary asked.

"I...I suppose so," I answered.

"So, we just need to figure out what it means, right?" Jennifer took over. "We need to solve it."

"We need to involve the police, is what we need to do," Sue said.

"Of course," I said.

John grabbed the phone in my hand, then started tapping on it.

"What are you doing, John?" Mary asked.

"I'm finding the rest of the verses," he said without looking up from the phone. "I can't afford to wait for no darn police." He paused, then looked up.

"Well, what does it say?" Jennifer asked.

He looked at me while he spoke. I don't know why.

"*One tumbled off and then there were eight.*"

"One tumbled off?" Mary repeated. "What does that mean?"

Now they were all looking at me for answers. I shrugged, feeling a huge amount of pressure on me.

"I...I don't know."

"But you've got to. We have to find out before it's too late," John said. "You've got to help us out."

"It was a little easier the first time," I said. "When the word home was actually mentioned...you know to find her at her...home..."

"It must mean she has fallen off of something, right?" Jennifer tried.

"Well, that's obvious, geez," Sue said. "No, there was a part at the beginning of the verse too. The part about the gate."

"*Nine little Injuns swingin' on a gate?*" I repeated.

"Yes," Sue said. "Does that ring a bell for anyone?"

"Do you have a gate at home?" I asked John.

He shook his head. "We have a wooden fence around our back-yard, but that's all. No gates."

I paused, then looked up. "There's a fence at the school. In the back by the playground facing the big trees. It has a gate."

CHAPTER FIFTY-TWO
May 2018

Never had two cars driven so fast down Minutemen Causeway and through the school zone, but that's what we did. Sue kept telling us to call the police, but I wasn't sure there was any time. I told her to do it on the way. The school was less than a minute down the road. We could make it there faster, and right now we had no time to waste.

As we reached the school, I parked the car in the grass, and we ran as fast as we could to the back side of the school, around the building till we spotted the fence and the gate in the back. We didn't have to look twice before we spotted her. On the fence, dressed in her hoodie that had the string tied in a bow at the neck, Emmy was dangling.

"Oh, my God," John exclaimed. "Oh, my God, Emmy, NO!"

He ran to her and grabbed her legs, then lifted her up against the iron gate. It was at least seven feet tall. Emmy wasn't responding. John was crying helplessly while I - ignoring the pain in my leg - climbed the gate and reached up for the string tied around her neck and pulled it off. The lifeless body of Emmy fell into her dad's arms, and he bent backward with her tightly hugged in his embrace, weeping.

"Call for an ambulance," I said as I managed to get back down, my leg in throbbing pain.

"It's coming with the police," Sue said, looking in despair at John with his daughter in his arms. "I figured we needed...one."

John sank to his knees with Emmy on top of him while I could hear the sirens wailing in the distance. I felt so helpless and couldn't stop crying.

"Is she...is she...?" Mary asked.

I shook my head. "I don't know."

John held his daughter tightly, and his crying suddenly stopped. He put his ear closer to her chest.

"I felt her heartbeat," he suddenly yelled, almost laughing. He fumbled and put a couple of fingers to the skin of her throat and pressed down.

"I feel a pulse," he said. "I feel a pulse; there's a pulse and a heartbeat. There was a heartbeat; I heard it!"

He put her down on the ground then looked at her face. "Emmy? Baby girl? Are you there? Baby?"

The girl lay lifelessly still, while her dad sobbed and laughed at the same time. He kept calling her name and soon the place was swarmed by police and paramedics, handling Emmy.

"I felt her heartbeat," John kept telling them like he wasn't sure they would believe him. Like he had to convince them she was actually still alive. "I felt it. When I put my ear to her chest. There was something like a small sound suddenly...like *tap-tap*. Just real quick and that's how I knew...she was still...I mean she is still...isn't she?"

The paramedic nodded without looking at John. Instead, he addressed his colleagues.

"I have a pulse, but she's barely breathing. We need to get her on support. Let's get the BVM ready."

We all watched, hugging one another, as John went with the ambulance and Emmy was rushed to Cape Canaveral Hospital. Holding one another, we were hoping and praying that she would survive this. Deep down, I couldn't help being slightly jealous of John. If Emmy survived this, then he had actually gotten his daughter back. The rest of us could only pray that we would be as lucky.

CHAPTER FIFTY-THREE

January 2000

The worst thing in Jane's life hadn't been her husband's beatings; it was the separation from her children. It turned out to be the most painful experience she ever had to endure. And soon the longing began to take a toll on her health as well. At the age of only twenty-eight, she suffered two heart attacks and was barely surviving the second one.

When she looked at herself in the mirror, she saw nothing but gray hair and beginning lines. She looked so tired, but barely even cared anymore. It wasn't like she was going to meet a new man, not that she was even looking. The idea of finding love was so far-fetched it almost made her laugh at her own reflection, had it not been so tragic. This was certainly not the life she had dreamt of when she had been lying in her bed at night as a teenager, fantasizing about her future.

She regained contact with her mother; that was the good part, and her mother helped her get her life back on track. She got a job at a local Walgreens and, with the money she made, she was soon able to pay rent for a small condo in Cocoa Beach, close to her children. She wasn't allowed any contact with them until she had gotten her life on track, they said, and after six months of separation, she was finally told she would be allowed to spend an hour with them, supervised, naturally.

Jane felt more excited to see them again than she had ever been for anything in her life. She also felt more nervous. Would the children remember her?

It was Colleen who brought them to her condo. Jane watched them drive up into the street below and watched while biting her nails as they got out of the car. Even Matthew was there in a car seat that Colleen carried out. Jane almost screamed when she saw them approach the front door and soon heard the buzz on the wall.

Jane rushed to it and buzzed them inside, then opened the front door, straightened her skirt, and took in a deep breath to calm herself down. The last thing she wanted to do was to throw herself at them when they arrived. She had to seem as normal as possible, as together as possible. Colleen would be watching her every move, listening to her every word, and inspecting the condo, checking her fridge, and looking for dirt and dust, Jane's mother had warned her.

"This is important if you want your kids back. You've got to be on your best behavior and look your most presentable. The hard part will not be when they arrive, but when they leave. You've got to let them go without crying or acting crazy, you hear me?"

She had heard her, and she remembered her words while standing at the top of the stairs, listening to her babies' voices approaching, butterflies flickering in her stomach. Everything inside of her wanted to scream their names, to run down toward them and grab them in her arms and never let go of them again. Ever.

But she couldn't. The children lived with Aunt Melissa and Uncle Jim now, and she had to accept that until things were changed. If she ever wanted them to change, this was her moment.

CHAPTER FIFTY-FOUR

May 2018

S une made dinner for me that night, and we ate together on the porch, listening to the waves crashing onto the beach. It was a gorgeous night out, and the moon rose from behind the ocean and stood like a white ball above our heads, lighting everything up. It always amazed me just how bright the moon shone here compared to at home. If I stood up, I actually cast a shadow.

Sune poured me a second glass of wine, and I smiled at him. The kids were done with their food. They grabbed their plates and went back inside.

"Nice evening, huh?" Sune said and pulled his chair close to mine. I nodded and looked up at the stars above us.

"How was your training today?" I asked, trying to think about something other than Julie.

"Really good. Dr. Herman says I'll be done in two months. I am at eighty-five percent of my mobility now. I even ran a little today, just for four minutes, but I ran, Rebekka. Can you believe it?"

"That's amazing, Sune," I said with half a chuckle. I was so thrilled for him, I really was, but it was hard to be happy in this situation. Sune noticed that my enthusiasm was pretty forced and put his hand on top of mine.

"I know it's hard. I just thought I'd tell you the good news."

"I know, sweetie, and I am truly happy. It's great. No, it's better than that; it's amazing news, honey. It's what we've hoped for for so long. I just wish…well, that Julie was here. I miss her so terribly; it almost hurts to even think about it. I can't stand having to spend yet another night without her. She's my daughter, Sune. She's my everything."

"Of course. You're scared. No wonder after what happened." He sipped his wine. "So, how's the girl. Will she survive?"

"Last I heard, yes. She's still unconscious, but stable. So that's good news."

"And what about the phone that they texted from? Could they track it?"

I shook my head. "I spoke to Jack earlier, and he said it was a dead end, unfortunately. The search after it sent them to a place an hour north of here, where they found the phone in a trash can. They say they're going to check for fingerprints, but if the kidnappers have gone to this much trouble in order for us not to trace it, then I have a feeling they won't be as careless as to leave fingerprints."

"You might have a point," he said.

"Jack is certain they will mess up at some point, though," I said. "He says they always do. I'm just not sure I want to sit here and wait for it, if you know what I mean."

"It's frustrating." Sune sipped his wine again.

"So, now what? We just wait again? Wait to see who's next, huh? How long till they reach *and then there were none*? Are you telling me all we can do is just sit here and wait? I mean, what do these people want from us? They've demanded no money or anything else. Do they just want to toy with us? Make us jump and run? What kind of sick people would do this? And what about us? Are we just supposed to sit here and let them toy with us in their sick game?"

"Is there anything else we can do?" Sune asked.

"That's what I want to know too. I want to get ahead of them somehow. But I don't know how. I tell you, I sometimes wish they would just torture it out of Mr. Meckler. If they're right and he is a part of it, then he must know more."

"Could you really live with yourself if you knew they tortured him?" Sune asked.

I shrugged. He had a point. I was against torture, but then again, this was my child. I would do anything to get information about where she was right now.

"What if the guy is innocent?" Sune asked.

I exhaled. "You're right. They've found nothing on his computer or at his house to connect him to the kidnapping. But still, maybe he's just really good at covering up. It is, however, bothering me that he's been in police custody while all this has been going on. I hardly think he's the mastermind behind it."

I finished my wine and asked for another glass. I needed it.

"There is one thing I'm pretty certain of, though," I then continued. "If it isn't Mr. Meckler, then it must be someone else from the school. Whoever planned this must have access to the parents' addresses and phone numbers, plus they had to know everything about how the dismissal procedure works. The letter to Nancy had no stamp on it; it was delivered personally when they placed the kid in the car, probably early in the morning. I think they're local. My guess is it's someone we know well."

CHAPTER FIFTY-FIVE

May 2018

They came back late at night. As the hatch opened, Alicia caught a brief glimpse of the moon before the pantyhose-covered face of a man appeared once again. He climbed down the ladder as a wave of fear rushed through the girls.

They had stopped believing that Alondra or Emmy would be coming back, and most of them inside the hot box truck feared being picked next. Alicia didn't know what to think about any of it. Like most of the girls, she feared the kidnappers were killing them off one by one, but then again, there was this small hope that maybe they weren't. It was Julie who had started it inside of her when the rest of them were freaking out. Julie had said that maybe they weren't being killed; maybe they were being sent home because their parents had paid the ransom. But did that mean that her parents hadn't paid for her yet? Why hadn't they?

Maybe they just haven't been told how or how much yet, she thought, calming herself down. *Maybe they're taking us one at a time.*

Alicia looked up at the man crawling down. Her hands were shaking lightly, but she tried to hide it by putting them behind her back. Trudy, who was sitting next to her on the dirty mattress, started to whimper and hid her face between her knees. They were all different in how they reacted, Alicia had noticed. Where some crept into the corners trying to hide, Alicia preferred to watch what was going on. She believed that it made a difference in who they ended up choosing, and maybe—just maybe—part of her wanted to be chosen this time. She almost tried to will it, to force it to happen. Because she was sick of this hot place; she was sick of feeling nauseous all the time, of fighting to not throw up because of the stench.

The kidnapper smiled and looked straight at her, and that was when she knew. Whatever she had done, whether it was looking at him or just by her will alone, she had made him choose her. Or maybe she just knew it was her turn and, when he pointed his finger at her, Alicia had already risen to her feet.

"You," he said. "Come with me."

Alicia smiled, excited to go, but also nervous as she grabbed onto the ladder and was about to climb after him.

"Alicia," a voice said behind her as several of the girls surrounded her. Alicia turned around and spotted Julie. Julie reached out her arms and pulled Alicia into a deep hug. Soon, most of the other girls followed. Even Tonya.

"I'll get help," Alicia whispered, her voice shivering. "If I survive, I'll come for you."

"Take care of yourself," Julie said, wiping tears from her eyes. Her lips were white and cracked.

"You too," Alicia said.

"Now!" the kidnapper said. "I don't have all night."

Julie let go of Alicia, and she started to climb. She could hear the girls whimpering below her. Some were crying, others just staring at her as she disappeared up toward the hole in the ceiling from where no one had returned so far.

The first thing Alicia did when her kidnapper closed the hatch behind her was to take in a deep breath, filling her lungs with the wondrous fresh air she had longed for for so long. She looked up at the starry sky, then began to cry at the gorgeous sight of the endless universe above her. All those stars and the gorgeous bright moon. So much space.

Just as she was about to take it all in, a blindfold was placed over her eyes, and the stars and limitless sky were gone once again.

CHAPTER FIFTY-SIX

January 2000

"Let me have a look at each and every one of you."

Jane looked into her children's faces. They were inside her small condo in the living room, sitting on her old brown couches she had bought for next to nothing on Craig's list. Colleen sat in a chair in the corner, observing their every move and listening in on every word.

"Gosh, you have all grown so much. How is that even possible in only six months?"

She was holding baby Matthew in her arms, keeping him close to her chest, just hugging him. He had learned how to sit and was almost crawling by now, she had been told.

"Well, he mostly pushes himself backward around the house; it's the darndest sight," Colleen had added when telling her.

Jane cried when thinking about how much she had missed already. She tried to hold it back, so Colleen wouldn't think that she couldn't keep herself together. Jane had to seem as healthy and normal as possible, but it was tougher than she had thought it would be.

A lot tougher.

"Anna, baby, how are you?" she asked and tried to address her.

But the girl would hardly look at her and kept turning her head away.

"What's wrong, baby?"

"They say it was your fault," Elisa said. "That dad hit her. You know…that day."

"But…but who would say such a thing?" Jane asked.

"Aunt Melissa and Uncle Jim. They say all kinds of stuff about you. Like how you can't take care of us and how you…"

Elisa received an elbow from her twin sister, Penelope, and stopped. Then she added:

"It's true, though."

Jane felt like someone had punched her in the stomach. Were they turning the kids against her? Her own children?

"But…surely none of you believe any of it…do you?" she asked. "Anna?"

But Anna still refused to look at her.

"They also say it's your fault that we have to live with them because you can't get your life together," Penelope said.

Matthew started to fuss in her arms and Jane tried to calm him down, but it didn't seem to help. Colleen straightened her back and gave her a look. Jane smiled comfortingly and tickled Matthew on the tummy, trying to calm him down, while singing his favorite song. The girls sat very still, and then Anna started to cry.

"What's wrong, baby? Oh, no, don't cry."

Jane turned to look at Elisa and told her to take Matthew for a few seconds, then grabbed Anna in her arms and hugged her.

"It's okay, baby. It's okay. I've missed you too. I've missed you all so much I can barely take it. I'm doing everything I can to get you back with me, do you hear me?"

Anna calmed down and sat in Jane's lap with a sniffle, rubbing her eyes. Jane pulled her into a close embrace when the girl winced with an *ouch*.

"What's wrong?"

Anna held her side like it was hurting.

"Have you hurt yourself?" Jane asked and pulled up Anna's

shirt. A big purple bruise was revealed. Jane could hardly breathe when she saw it.

"Who did this?" Jane asked angrily.

None of the children replied. "Who did this?" Jane said, raising her voice a little too much. "Who did it? Was it Aunt Melissa? Uncle Jim? Your dad? Have you been seeing your father?"

Colleen was on her feet now, walking to her.

"I think this is enough for today."

"Have you seen this?" Jane asked and showed her the bruise. "Have you seen what they've done to my baby girl?"

Colleen sighed. "She could have gotten that from playing in the yard or at a playground. Melissa and Jim have been very good to the children. We visit them regularly, and the children are all thriving in their home."

"They're thriving? Thriving? That doesn't look much like thriving to me? This is abuse, Colleen, can't you see it? You, of all people, should recognize it. I can't believe you. You place my kids in care with some people they hardly know, and now they're allowed to abuse them? I can't...I can't even begin to...How can you let this..."

Colleen turned away from her and started to gather the children. "This is exactly the kind of hostile behavior we can't tolerate..."

Jane grabbed her by the arm. "They are my kids. These people are hurting my children!"

"You're making me very nervous right now," Colleen said and glanced at Jane's hand still grabbed around her arm. "I'll call the police if I have to. Don't force me to call them. You'll end up never seeing your kids again. This is not a joke, Jane."

Jane let go with a snort. Colleen gathered the children and took Matthew in her arms.

Seeing this, Jane realized she had messed up. She felt desperate, almost panicking at the thought of them leaving again.

"Wait," she said. "Can I just give him a kiss before you leave? Just one little kiss? Please?"

Colleen paused for a second, her back still turned to Jane.

"Please? I don't know when I'll see him again. Please?" Jane folded her hands and began to cry. She couldn't say goodbye to her kids already. She couldn't bear to see them leave. How was she supposed to survive this? How was she supposed to go on when she had no idea when she would see them and hold them again? Especially Matthew, who was still so young. The longing to be close to him was agonizing. It was killing her.

Colleen sighed deeply, then looked down at the girls. For a second, Jane was certain she would turn around and let her hold Matthew and kiss him one last time before they left, but she didn't. Instead, she said:

"Come on, kids. We need to get you home now."

CHAPTER FIFTY-SEVEN
May 2018

I actually slept a little. I hadn't expected to since I was so worried, but I had at least four hours of sleep and, when I woke up, I couldn't stop wondering what this day was going to bring. Would there be another one? Another note or text? Would it be Julie this time?

Before going to bed, I had stared at the lyrics of the nursery rhyme, and I was singing them out loud to myself in bed.

"Eight little Injuns gayest under heav'n.
One went to sleep
And then there were seven;"

Sune was still sleeping, and fortunately, I didn't wake him up by singing it over and over again, wondering what it would mean in the minds of some sick psycho kidnappers. How would they use it? If only I could guess that, then we could get ahead of them. The biggest problem was that I didn't even know what child would be next.

The door to our bedroom opened, and William stormed in, then jumped onto our bed, laughing and fooling around. I gave him a big kiss, then grabbed him and held him in a close embrace.

"Ju-Ju comin' home today?" he asked.

I exhaled and ruffled his hair. "I'm afraid that I don't know, big guy. We can only hope."

He tilted his head. "Mommy worried."

"Yes, your mom is worried," I said. "I want her to come home. I miss her. Don't you miss her?"

He looked like he was contemplating the question for a few seconds, then nodded.

"Good. I'm glad you miss her too. She's your sister, you know."

William shrugged, then jumped on Sune, who woke up with a roar. Will sat on his face with his wet diaper and Sune laughed, then grabbed him and lifted him off.

"Someone needs to get out of his diaper," he chuckled. William only used a diaper at night, and it was usually filled to the brim once he woke up after a long night's sleep.

Sune got out of bed and, almost without even limping or struggling, walked to the changing table where he removed William's diaper. I enjoyed watching him being almost back to normal. To think that a small thing like changing a diaper could be such a big deal, but it was to Sune. He loved being able to take care of things around the house again, to take care of the kids and me. And I enjoyed watching him do it with such pride.

"There we go," he said and lifted William down to the floor. "Good as new."

William squealed and then ran off.

"Who could have known that watching you remove a wet diaper would turn me on so much?" I asked.

He approached me, then crawled under the covers. He kissed me gently, then looked into my eyes.

"My legs aren't the only thing around here that has regained its mobility, you know," he said. "You want to? It's been a while?"

I stroked his hair gently, then sighed. "I...I can't. I'm sorry."

Sune's eyes lost their sparkle. He moved away from me.

"Okay. I get it."

I felt bad. "It's not because of you," I said. "I just...I can't with all that's been going on...you know with Julie and all the worry and..."

"It's been two years, Rebekka. Two and a half, actually. I'm beginning to think you lost interest in me. I could understand it if I was still stuck in that chair like I was for two years, but now that I'm not? Now that I'm actually capable of…"

"Sune, my daughter is missing. I can't just pretend like she isn't. I'm in pain. I'm sick with worry; how do you want me to…?"

He rose to his feet. "Just forget about it, Rebekka. I'll make us some breakfast."

CHAPTER FIFTY-EIGHT

May 2018

We ate breakfast outside under the umbrella. Sune made pancakes and bacon for us all, and for once, I actually ate some. I still couldn't stop worrying about this day and what it might bring, but I tried not to ruin everything by letting it affect me. Sune seemed to be still upset, but I couldn't really deal with him right now.

After the boys were done eating, they grabbed a ball and ran down to the beach to play soccer, while I cleaned up. My wound in my thigh was still swollen and ugly, but it didn't hurt much anymore. It was healing very nicely, even though it was going to leave an ugly scar. I was going in for a checkup in a couple of days, but I felt sure that they were going to tell me it looked great.

Sune was already in the kitchen when I brought in the plates. He grabbed them from me and put them in the dishwasher. Then he leaned over and kissed me softly. He looked into my eyes, his showing deep concern for me.

"I know this is tough, Rebekka. I also know that I don't know exactly how tough it is. I can only imagine. But if it is any consolation, I think you're doing great; I really do."

He turned around and poured me some more coffee, then

handed the cup to me.

"Thanks," I said and sipped it, relieved that he wasn't angry with me. I needed him right now. I needed him to understand me. "The worst part is the waiting. I mean, I'm pretty sure one of us will get a message somehow today, right? What if it's me? What if I get the message? What if I get the riddle and need to go find Julie some-where, not knowing if she will still be alive? What if I'm too late?"

"You won't be, Rebekka," Sune said and closed the dishwasher.

"How can you be so certain?"

He leaned over and kissed me again, then looked into my eyes. "Because I know you, Rebekka. Now...should we go check the mailbox together?"

"I already checked it," I said. "At two o'clock in the morning and then again at six and right before you woke up. But I need to check it again and, this time, it would be nice if we could do it together. I don't want to find the letter alone. I keep checking my phone for messages too, fearing the worst, jumping at every vibra-tion it makes. It's silly. I don't even know how the kidnappers will get the next message out. They might even use a flippin' Pigeon Post for all I know."

Sune smiled. "Let's do it together. Come."

We walked out the front door, just as I spotted Sue Porter rushing up toward our house. By the look on her pale face, I knew this day it wasn't going to be my turn.

It was hers.

"Oh, dear Lord, Sue. Is it Alicia?"

"I...I just...I was checking the mail, you know...fearing to find a letter like Nancy did, but then my phone...it vibrated, and there was a phone call...it was Alicia's voice. She was singing...you know the song, the rhyme. But only one line from it. It sounded like a recording, because once it was done, it was repeated, and then they hung up."

"Let me guess," I said. "The line she sang was *Eight little Injuns gayest under heav'n*, right?"

Sue nodded. "I...I don't know what to do. Rebekka, please help me like you helped John. Please, just help me!"

CHAPTER FIFTY-NINE

May 2018

Julie couldn't believe that Alicia was gone. She kept glaring toward the hatch above her, wondering if she would ever see her again. Nikki moved in her corner, and Julie tended to her. She grabbed a bottle of water and realized they were running out quickly. The same went for the cereal and crackers. There were lots of empty boxes but very few full ones. Would they bring them new supplies soon?

Maybe they don't even care if we starve down here since we'll be dead soon anyway?

Julie felt so tired. Yet, somehow, something else seemed to be growing inside of her now, a spark of some sort that had lingered inside of her ever since Alicia had left.

Anger.

Julie was angry. She was sick and tired of being a prisoner, of leaving her entire existence and her future in the hands of some sick bastards who, for all she knew, could be pedophiles. They could be selling the girls off to a life in slavery in what she had heard grownups refer to as trafficking.

She was sick of them deciding whether she should live or die, whether she was going to see her mother or not.

Nikki moaned in her sleep, and Julie rushed to her, put a hand on her forehead, then retracted it quickly. Nikki was burning hot, even worse than she had been earlier. The fever was rising, and Nikki was deeper in the land of the dead than that of the living.

If you don't do something, she'll die.

Julie put the water bottle against Nikki's lips and tried to pour the liquid into her mouth, but it ran down the sides of her mouth.

"Drink, dang it!" Julie said, a sense of deep dread overpowering her. Nikki had barely taken in any water over the past twenty-four hours. If she didn't drink soon, she would die. No one could survive without water. That much she knew.

Julie tried to lift Nikki's head up to make the passageway more open, then poured more water into her mouth, but the water simply ran back out, and she had no idea if Nikki even got anything inside her stomach at all.

Julie put her down again, then put her ear close to Nikki's face.

She's barely breathing!

Julie grabbed Nikki's wrist and felt for a pulse but could hardly feel it. It was there, but it was just very, very weak.

Julie felt it as her own pulse went up. The thought of not being able to save Nikki was crushing. Besides, Nikki wasn't the only one who had a fever by now. She wasn't going just to sit there and let them all die one after another. Second grade Aubrey had been coughing and broke into a fever the night before. She too was sleeping heavily most of the time now.

Julie rose to her feet, then drank the rest of the water from her own bottle. She threw the empty bottle in the pile, then walked to the hatch and looked up, mumbling to herself.

"We have to get out of here. Now. There has to be a way. There simply has to be."

It was when looking down at her feet and at what she was standing on that Julie realized that maybe there was and maybe they had been sitting on the solution the entire time.

CHAPTER SIXTY

May 2018

O*ne went to sleep and then there were seven.*
That was the line that kept buzzing in my mind. That
was the riddle we had to solve before it was too late. At first, I had
thought it was simple enough. She had to be somewhere sleeping,
maybe even in her own bed, like we had found Alondra in her own
garage. But we had already checked that and found nothing in her
entire house.

I had called Jack Ryder and filled him in. He was sitting with us
now and kept rubbing his forehead and running his hand through
his long curly surf hair. He had all his patrols on high alert, driving
around Cocoa Beach, looking for Alicia, but so far, we had no idea
where to even begin looking for her.

"Maybe we need to look at the first line in the verse too," I said
and pressed the display on my phone. I found the lyrics once again.
My fingers were trembling. I couldn't stand the wait or the pressure.
I couldn't stand the thought that every minute mattered; every
second that passed could mean that we were too late to save her.

It was brutal.

"Eight little Injuns gayest under heav'n?" Jack asked.

"Yes, that has to mean something too, right?" I asked. "Like it did with Emmy."

Jack nodded. "Makes sense."

I stared at Sue. She had that look on her face that terrified me. She hadn't uttered a word in a long time. Her husband Emmett was standing by the fireplace, sipping a glass of whiskey. All I knew about him was that he was a highly esteemed judge, and it was obvious he was used to people doing what he told them to. Every now and then, he would get mad at Jack and tell him that *if anything happened to his little girl, he would make sure he would never work again.*

Jack was good at handling him, I was surprised to see. I'm not sure I could have remained so calm had he spoken to me like that. But not Jack. He spoke to him in a calm voice and let him know that the entire police department was on this case; everyone was doing all they could, and he would personally do his best to get his daughter home.

"But what does it mean?" Jack said.

"Gayest under heav'n," I said. "That must translate to the happiest place on earth, right?"

Jack's glare met mine and our eyes locked for a second.

"Well, there really is only one place it can be, then…right?" he said.

I nodded. Jack grabbed his phone and dialed a number. "I'll get ahold of Orange County's Sherriff department. They can get there faster." He put the phone to his ear and walked away. I sat in a chair next to Sue and held her hands in mine.

"We'll find her. Don't worry. We'll get her."

I gave her a smile, trying to be as comforting as possible, secretly praying that when they found her, it would be in time. Disney World was a big place, after all.

CHAPTER SIXTY-ONE

May 2018

J ulie grabbed a mattress and pulled it across the floor. She lifted the edge of it and then placed it on top of the first one. It was hard to breathe in the hot and humid air, and she ran out of breath very fast. Yet soon she had stacked five mattresses on top of one another. The other girls—those who were still awake and not feverish or too weak—helped her get the sixth one up there as well and, soon, they had built a tower.

To get the last mattress on top of it, Julie had to crawl up and pull it up. Then, as she stood on top of the tower, she stretched as far as she could and realized she could easily touch the hatch.

Why on earth hadn't they thought of this before? They had all been too sick with worry and paralyzed by fear to think about escaping. But now that Julie was touching the bottom of the hatch, she felt that spark of hope return. She reached her hands up and placed them both on the bottom of the hatch, then pressed with all her strength.

The metal plate didn't move.

"What's happening, Julie? Can you open it?" Haley asked.

Julie grunted and tried again. The metal plate still didn't move. It was too heavy.

"It's like there's something on top of it," she said, panting. "Something heavy."

Julie groaned, then gave up and sat down on the mattresses. The other girls were looking up at her, eyes filled with anticipation. How could she let them down?

"I can't," she mumbled to herself. "Not when we're this close."

Julie made a loud growl, then pressed her shoulder against the metal plate and tried with all her weight to lift it up. For the first time, the metal plate actually moved. Not much, but just a little bit. Enough for Julie to laugh and allow herself to be filled with hope.

"It moved," she yelled to the others. She had to stop and catch her breath and sat back on the mattress. "The plate moved."

The girls below her let out small shrieks of joy and laughter. Julie looked down at them from her tower.

You can't let them down now.

Then she rose to her feet and pressed using her shoulder again. The plate moved a little more but now a bunch of dirt fell onto her face, and she had to let herself fall back, spitting and rubbing it out of her eyes.

"What happened?" Haley asked.

Julie looked up at the plate above her. "It's dirt. They covered the plate with dirt. That's why it's so heavy. The bastards buried us."

The very thought filled Julie with claustrophobia.

"Can you get it to open?" Tonya asked.

Julie looked down at them. "I…I don't think so. There could be several feet of dirt up there. I think we're pretty far underground."

Trudy let out a shriek. Julie looked at Nikki, who lay motionless in the corner.

No, she couldn't give up now. There was no time to waste. Nikki had to get out, and it had to be now.

Julie felt the mattress beneath her. It was old and worn. The springs were poking out in places, but so was something else. Julie felt it with her hand, sized it up, then used her nails to rip the molded fabric open. Then she pulled out a wooden stick. Happily, she felt the mattress and found more. Two…three more. Then she looked down at Haley and Tonya, the two strongest and healthiest among them.

"Get up here, girls. We're going to start digging."

CHAPTER SIXTY-TWO

June 2000

"All rise, the Court is now in session."

Jane had finally been able to afford a good lawyer. Not an excellent one, but a decent one, one that believed she had a case that could help her get her children back. She had saved every penny she made working two jobs and, with her mom's help, she finally had enough money.

The past six months, she had only seen her children once a month, but she quickly came to dread the visits. They were so short, and saying goodbye made her feel like screaming in anger. It was awful. Colleen watched them like a hawk, taking notes on how she and the kids behaved together. But worst of all was that the kids began saying terrible things about her. They said that their aunt had told them that Jane was bad, that she was a drug addict, that she didn't want them back.

And every time, at least one of them had shown visible signs of abuse. Yet the DCF had refused to act, even though Jane constantly pointed out that her children were suffering. The worst part was that the children were covering for their aunt and uncle or maybe even their father since Jane didn't know if they were seeing him, but she had a feeling they were. But whoever was abusing them, they didn't want to tell her who it was. And that meant they didn't want to tell the DCF either. Every week, Jane called Colleen, asking her if she had looked into it, and every time, she received the same answer.

"We do our visits twice a month, and the children are fine. The bruises are from playing roughly in the yard. The children even confirmed they were themselves."

All Jane had been able to do so far was to stand by and watch. Meanwhile, the DCF had canceled future visits since they didn't think she was fit to have visits with the children because of her temper, which they assumed was alcohol or drug-related. Where they came up with all those lies was beyond Jane.

But now she was ready to fight back. She was going to get her children back, no matter how long she had to keep at it.

Her lawyer, Scott, stood up and began to tell her story. He then argued why he believed she should be allowed to have her children back with her.

"She has done everything the DCF has asked for and even more. She has taken drug tests, and they showed up negative. She's healthy and has two good jobs with good pay. Her mother will even help out if needed. It is time for her to be reunited with her children."

Much to Jane's surprise, the judge agreed that Jane should be reunited with her youngest. Since the child was still so young, he needed his mother more than anyone, was his argument.

Jane couldn't stop smiling as they handed her Matthew, who was now one year old and able to stand and walk on his own. He clung to his mother, and she couldn't stop kissing him. She was never letting go of him again.

It wasn't much; it wasn't what she dreamt of, but it was a start, it was her first victory.

CHAPTER SIXTY-THREE

May 2018

The gayest place under the heavens...the gayest place.
I couldn't find rest, even after Jack left and he told us Orange County's Sheriff's Department was all over Disney, looking for Alicia, and that it was only a matter of time before they would find her.

There was something about all this that made me uneasy. I couldn't quite put my finger on it. It was mostly the fact that in the two previous incidents, the girls had been hidden locally. Disney was far away and maybe just a tad too obvious.

What if that was what the kidnappers wanted us to think?

I had promised Sue to stay with her till they received news from the police, and so now I was sitting in her house, tapping my fingers uneasily on the long solid wooden dinner table they had once told me they had shipped to their house from Bali, Indonesia. It weighed sixteen hundred pounds Emmett had told me back when I had the tour of their house when we had been in Florida for just a little over a month.

"Took eight big men to lift it inside," Emmett said and knocked on it. "Guess we're not moving anywhere soon, ha-ha."

Back then, I had admired the table, but right now it seemed too big, too long, and too empty. This type of table required a big family and, most of all, children around it. It was macabre, but I couldn't stop wondering if they would ever sit around it as a family again.

I got up and walked to Sue, who was standing by the kitchen sink, looking out the window, nervously rubbing her hands against each other. Next to her on the counter was her phone that she glared at anxiously every few seconds. But it remained black.

"What if it isn't the happiest place," I mumbled, standing next to her. Outside the window, I spotted a lizard that looked like it was enjoying the sun.

The thought had lingered in the back of my mind for several minutes now, and I couldn't hold it in anymore. I couldn't stand the thought that maybe they were looking in the wrong place.

Sue gasped and looked at me. "Don't say that."

"I'm sorry. I just can't stop thinking…"

"What do you mean?"

I shrugged. "I could be wrong. It's just…"

"What?"

"Well…what if they actually mean the *gayest* place, not the happiest."

"You mean as in gay and lesbian gay?" she asked, surprised. "But that makes no sense."

"Maybe not." I paused, then continued. "Still, there is always that little *what if* in the back of your mind, right? I mean, I could be wrong, but…"

"You could also be right, and we can't afford to risk that right now," Sue said. "Tell me more."

"The only thing I can think of is a gay bar," I said.

"A gay bar, huh? The only one I know of around here is the Electric Lounge. It's only five minutes down the road," she said. "Right off 520."

I grabbed her car keys and looked at her. "Let me drive. You're too upset."

CHAPTER SIXTY-FOUR
May 2018

The place was closed at this time of day. From the outside, it didn't look like much. A couple of masked and dressed up mannequins in the window made me think it might as well have been a clothing store as a bar lurking behind them. The door wasn't locked, and we walked inside, into the darkness.

"Hello?"

A woman with heavy makeup and her long black hair put up in a ponytail came out, looking at us suspiciously.

"We're closed."

I paused. I had no idea how to explain any of this to a stranger. Where did you even begin? We didn't have much time.

"I am sorry," I said.

"You lost?" she asked, chewing her gum.

"Not exactly," I said. "I mean…this is going to sound really strange, but we're looking for a little girl."

Sue stepped up and showed her the picture of Alicia from her phone. "She's my daughter," she said. "You might have seen her picture on the news."

"What? She run away or somethin'?" the woman asked, the piercing in her nose vibrating as she spoke.

"She was taken," Sue said. "Along with nine other girls from the same school."

"Oh, okay. I think I heard about that, yeah. Well, I haven't seen her; I'm sorry," she said then looked like she expected us to leave.

"The thing is…" I said. "We have reason to believe she might be here…somewhere. In here."

The woman gave me another suspicious look. I couldn't blame her. "In here? You do realize what this place is, right?"

I nodded. "That's kind of why."

The woman shook her head. "I don't know…it sounds very fishy…I think we would have noticed if there was a young girl in here somewhere. It's not who usually comes here, if you know what I mean."

"We know," Sue said. "And it might not even be here, but could we please take a look around?"

She looked skeptical. "Are the police involved?"

I shook my head. "I mean they are, but not in this part of it. They're searching elsewhere. We just had this idea…Listen, I know it sounds crazy…but we…"

"Crazy as a bat," she exclaimed. "None of what you two are saying is making any sense to me."

"It doesn't have to. All we want is to look around a little bit, can we do that?" Sue asked hopefully.

The woman shrugged. "Sure. But you won't find her here."

"We'll take that chance. Thank you," I said.

The woman returned to her small office, and we started our search. The bar wasn't very big, so it was easy to see that she wasn't in the main area.

"I'll check the bathrooms," I said and hurried into the back. I opened the door and peeked inside one of the bathrooms. It was very nicely decorated with pictures of Marilyn Monroe and Joan Crawford, but there was no Alicia. I opened the door to the next one, but I didn't even get to peek inside before the woman from earlier suddenly yelled at us.

"Come out here!"

I rushed back into the bar where a guy was standing with Alicia in his arms. Sue let out a loud scream before she ran to her.

"Brian found her in the back," the woman said, her voice shaking. "By the trash cans. She was inside of one, he said. Who would do something like that to a child?"

"Alicia, it's Mommy, please, please, baby, wake up," Sue cried and tried to grab her daughter from Brian's arms. The young man stared at her, completely paralyzed.

"Is she breathing?" I asked.

Sue tried to hold onto her daughter but had to put her down. She was weeping helplessly and calling her daughter's name.

I knelt next to her, then felt her throat for a pulse. It was there, but very, very weak.

"She's alive," I said.

"But why isn't she waking up, Rebekka? Why isn't she waking up? What did they do to her? To my poor girl?"

I looked at the girl's face, then remembered the verse from the nursery rhyme.

"She's sleeping," I said. "They must have slipped her sleeping pills to get her to fall into a deep sleep."

"Sleeping pills? But...but how many?" Sue asked, her voice turning shrill and anxious.

I looked at Alicia's jeans. Something was poking out of her pockets. I pulled it out. It was two jars of sleeping pills.

"You think they gave her all those?" Sue shrieked and clung to her daughter. "That's enough to kill her!"

"That it is," I said.

"But...but...so it was all in vain? We were too late?" Sue asked.

"We don't know that yet," I said. "We don't know how far the pills have made it into her system. If there are any left in her stomach, we have to get them out now. We have to make her throw up."

Sue didn't hesitate for even a second. She plunged three fingers into her daughter's throat and forced them down so far that the sparse contents of the girl's stomach soon landed on the dance floor. Luckily, they had given her lots of water to flush down the pills, and it made it easier for them to come back up. Sue continued to make her daughter throw up, while I called for an ambulance and alerted Jack Ryder. By the time the paramedics arrived, Alicia had begun groaning and, once she was on the stretcher being rolled into the ambulance, she opened her eyes and looked at her mother.

CHAPTER SIXTY-FIVE
May 2018

They had to hurry. They had to make it out of there before the kidnappers came for the next girl. Julie didn't really know exactly how much time she had left, but she sensed they were cutting it close. Her arms were sore from the digging, and she had dirt everywhere. In her mouth, nostrils, and even in her ears. Yet, she still kept going. With all her strength, she dug out more dirt and let it fall into the coffin. Haley and Tonya were still by her side, digging as well, and soon they felt the dirt get looser and looser and it was easier to remove it.

Until it happened. Until they finally broke through it and felt the fresh air hit their faces and their eyes looked up at the sky above. The sun was getting ready to set in the distance, and the coming darkness would provide an excellent cover for them to get away. It also meant the kidnappers would be here again soon since it was always dark above them when they opened the hatch.

"We did it," she exclaimed and took in a long, deep breath before she spoke again with some tired, yet light, laughter. "We totally did it."

Haley and Tonya came up behind her and looked into the

orange sky above them. Haley stepped up and crawled out of the hole.

"Let's get out of here."

"We need to get the others," Julie said and looked down.

Nikki hadn't moved for a very long time, and it worried her. She had been keeping an eye on her while digging, glancing down at her every now and then, hoping and praying she would be all right, that she would stay alive while they dug their way out.

"There's no time," Haley said. "The kidnappers will be back soon, and then it will all have been in vain."

Tonya crawled out as well and stood next to Haley, looking down at Julie. "We can run for help. We can come back."

Julie crawled out too. She wanted to laugh when she felt the wind on her face. Then she glanced down at the girls below her. Several of them were sick and probably wouldn't be able to run much. Still. There was no way she would ever leave them here. Trudy and Britney had already started to climb the mattresses to get up. Julie looked down at them.

"Help me get the others up as well. The sick ones might need to be carried," Julie said and turned to look at Haley and Tonya for help.

They weren't there.

They had already taken off and were running toward the trees in the far distance, heading for the swamps. Julie sighed, then looked down at the girls climbing up toward her, frantically clinging onto the mattresses, their eyes fixed on the opening and the freedom awaiting them. Julie couldn't blame them. She too wanted to run away most of all but how could she? She couldn't just leave the sick ones behind.

As Britney and Trudy made it to the opening, she helped them get up and out. They squealed in joy, then took off running toward the tall trees in the distance where the others had disappeared to as well. Julie looked down into the hole where the last two girls were. Aubrey was sitting up, looking toward her. She was weak.

Julie swallowed hard, wondering if she dared to go all the way down there and help them. It was a great risk. She looked toward the swamps where the others had already disappeared. If she ran now, she would make it too. But where did that leave Aubrey and Nikki?

They'll kill them, won't they? When they realize we're all gone, they'll have to get rid of them.

Julie didn't dare to take the chance. She took one last breath of fresh air, then glanced toward the forest before she let herself sink back into the hole, into the stuffy unbreathable air and eye-watering stench and landed on top of the pile of dirty mattresses.

CHAPTER SIXTY-SIX

May 2018

It was with a strange empty feeling that I returned to the beach house and my family. William greeted me with a warm hug, while Tobias and Sune were playing some game on the Xbox and hardly even noticed I came home. I didn't want to disturb them, so I walked to the kitchen and poured myself some coffee. As I lifted the cup toward my mouth, I realized my hand was shaking so heavily I could barely hold it still.

I put it down with a deep sigh, then began to cry. I sat on the barstool at the breakfast counter and hid my face between my hands and let the tears roll down my cheeks, sobbing helplessly.

"Mommy cryin'!" William yelled and ran to his dad. "Daaaad! Mommy crying!"

Sune gave up on whatever he was playing and rushed toward me. He sat next to me and put an arm around my shoulder.

"What's wrong, Rebekka? I thought you found the girl? You told me so on the phone? You said you found her and that she was alive?"

I sniffled and wiped away my tears, trying hard to look normal. "We did," I said.

"Then why are you crying? Isn't that a happy thing?" Sune asked.

"Mommy worried about Ju-Ju," William exclaimed, addressed toward his dad, placing his hands on his hips.

It made me chuckle.

"He's right," I said. "I just...I'm so happy for Sue and John and all that. They have their little girls back, but I still don't have mine. And tomorrow, I have to go through all this once again. Will it be Julie this time? Or will I have to go through trying to get to another parent's girl, worrying that we'll be too late before it's finally my turn? And will I be able to find her? I can't stand having to wait like this, feeling like I'm in some stupid video game and that soon I will lose and that stupid sign will flash GAME OVER."

Sune sighed. I could tell he was searching for words to say. I looked into his eyes.

"I'm sorry," I said. "I'm pulling you down. You were having fun. How did your training go today?"

"Amazing," he said, almost laughing. "I'm getting better and better every day. These people really know what they're doing."

"That's wonderful," I said. I know it didn't sound like it, but I actually meant it. It was so great that he was improving. That was why we were here in the first place.

Sune placed a hand on my shoulder, then leaned over and kissed my cheek. "You'll get her home. I know you will."

"I just wish...that I could somehow get ahead of these bastards. The next line in the rhyme is *Seven little Injuns cuttin' up their tricks. One broke his neck and then there were six.*" I looked at Sune like I expected a certain reaction, then continued.

"What is that supposed to mean? They'll break Julie's neck? Is that going to give me a chance to save her? Or will she end up like Alondra? Because breaking your neck...that is pretty definite. Either you'll never walk again, or you'll die, right?"

"Maybe we shouldn't go down that road yet," Sune said. "We don't even know if she's the one who's next. And, hey, maybe Alicia can tell you something that will lead to them being found, huh? Maybe it won't come to that."

I sipped my coffee, finally being able to keep my hand still enough, but it didn't even taste good. Sune looked into my eyes. I so deeply hoped he was right, but it was getting increasingly harder for me to keep my hopes up. Today had been another close call. We couldn't afford any more of those.

CHAPTER SIXTY-SEVEN

May 2018

J ulie grabbed Aubrey first. Luckily, she was light, and Julie could easily lift her. She carried her to the mattresses, then lifted her up as far as she could stretch, so Aubrey could grab onto the sides and pull herself up with her arms. Julie pushed her from beneath while Aubrey pulled and pulled. When she could tell Aubrey was almost out of strength, Julie climbed up further and pushed her upward, then crawled up further and pushed her again till Aubrey was finally at the top of the pile and could lie down on top.

Julie crawled up to her.

"You're almost there," she said. "But we must hurry. They could be back anytime now."

Aubrey stared at the dark sky above them. She was lying on her back, panting. Then she began to cry.

"I can't. Not anymore. I'm so tired."

"You can't give up now," Julie said. "Look how close you are to freedom. All you have left is to crawl up through the tunnel we dug. You can do it. I know you can."

Aubrey couldn't stop crying. Julie didn't know what to do. She looked down at Nikki, who was still motionless on the floor. The kidnappers couldn't be far away now.

"Come on, Aubrey, please," she begged. "I'll help you the last part. Just…you have to do some work yourself too; will you, please?"

"I can't! I can't!" Aubrey cried. "I'm too tired."

Julie looked up at the sky above, then cleared her throat. She thought about the many times she had to deal with her baby brother being all whiney and not wanting to do what he was told, especially when he was tired and cranky. There was usually no reasoning with him at that point. Just like then, this moment required action.

"I don't have time for this," Julie said and grabbed Aubrey in her arms. She lifted the squealing child up toward the hole, then bent her arms down and threw her up. Aubrey screamed, then grabbed the edge of the hole and hung there, crying.

"Help!"

Julie stood on her tippy toes, then stretched her arms up and managed to push Aubrey the last part of the way. Aubrey soon peeked down at her. She had stopped crying.

"Now, run," Julie said. "I know you're sick; I know you're tired, but you have to get away. Run or walk or even crawl if you have to. Get away as fast as you can. Get to the tall trees and hide. I'll come right after you. I need to get Nikki too."

Aubrey nodded, then gave Julie one last glare before she disappeared. Julie looked down at Nikki in the back with an exhale. She was so exhausted; it seemed almost impossible to climb all the way down there once again and get another little girl all the way up.

But it had to be done. Julie let herself slide down onto the mattresses, then jumped into the box truck and landed on the floor. But she didn't land right on her foot, and she tumbled onto the dirty floor with a twisted ankle.

Julie growled in pain but got up and stood on it even though it hurt. She had no time for pain. She looked at Nikki, then rushed to her, trying to put as little weight on the ankle as possible. She sat next to the tiny girl, then grabbed her into her arms, turned, and looked at the tower of mattresses in front of her, wondering how she was going to get Nikki all the way up there. With Aubrey, it had been hard, and she had even been able to help. Nikki wasn't awake. She couldn't pull herself up with her arms the way Aubrey had.

There has to be a way. There has to be some way.

Without even thinking about how she was going to do it, Julie simply took off toward the mattresses, Nikki clutched in her arms. She held her the way she had learned in swimming lessons that you had to hold someone you were rescuing, with one arm around her chest, then with the other she pulled herself—and Nikki—upward. Fighting, pressing through the pain in her foot and body, forgetting hunger and thirst along with weakness and exhaustion, she pulled and pulled, and finally managed to get herself up to the top of the mattresses, then swung Nikki up onto them before crawling up herself. Panting and almost choking, she looked up through the hole above them.

"We're almost there, Nikki. We're almost there! Look at the sky above us. Look at the beautiful sky!"

Julie turned to look up herself when she heard agitated voices coming from aboveground. Before she knew it, someone peeked down at her.

"What the heck?"

The confused eyes were scrutinizing her. Julie held her breath. Their eyes locked for a few seconds, hers pleading, his flickering while he figured out what was going on. Next, he reached inside the tunnel, grabbed the hatch, and slammed it shut.

CHAPTER SIXTY-EIGHT

May 2018

I stopped the car outside the school and got out. It was dark, and I could barely see the entrance. I walked up to it and tried to open the door, but it was locked. Then I walked around the building back where the playground was. I used my flashlight to light up the area. At first, I shone it on the gate, remembering with a shiver where Emmy had hung. I stared at the gate for a few seconds, while images of her rushed through my mind, bringing me back for a few seconds to that awful day before I moved on. I walked to the slide and shone my flashlight on it. The slide was always Julie's favorite part of any playground. She could keep going on that thing forever and ever. She loved it way more than the swings, which were what most kids—especially girls—preferred. But that was Julie for you. Always had a mind of her own. Marched to the beat of her own drum.

I thought I heard a sound, then turned around and shone my flashlight in the direction of it, and as I did, a shadow rushed through the beam of light and disappeared between the trees behind the playground.

"Hello? Is anyone here?"

My voice had a shiver to it as I spoke.

"Hello?"

The shadow returned and ran past the beam again with what I believed sounded like a giggle, then disappeared behind the slides as I tried to follow it with the light.

"Who's there?"

Another sound came from behind me, and I turned to shine my flashlight at it, but the shadow was too fast. The hand holding my flashlight was shaking and the beam trembling as it hit the dangling swings. There was a sense of deep dread inside me that I couldn't shake. Somehow, I just knew something bad was about to happen, something terrifying.

"Who are you?"

The giggling sound was back, this time to my left, and I turned the flashlight and shone it on a face. The sight of it made me cry in relief.

"Julie!"

She was standing between the swings, not moving a muscle. I began to cry. "Julie? Is that really you? Julie?"

I approached her, shining my light on her, walking closer and closer, my heart pounding so terribly in my chest it almost hurt.

Why isn't she moving? Why isn't she saying anything?

"Julie?"

I walked closer, and now I could see her eyes. She was staring at me, but she didn't seem to react. It was like she was looking right through me. I rushed to her and grabbed her in my arms.

"Oh, Julie. Oh, dear Julie, you have no idea how happy I am to see you, baby. Oh, baby girl. I was so scared."

I held her in a close embrace, then realized her body felt completely limp in my arms. I put her down and looked into her face. Her eyes were looking at me like they couldn't recognize me, blinking and moving, telling me she was alive.

"Julie, it's me. It's your mother. Why aren't you saying anything? Julie?"

As she turned to look away, her head tilted sideways, detaching itself from her throat. Her head was now dangling from her shoulder, only attached to her body by a pulsing vein. The sound of the blood pumping through it was so loud it hurt my ears.

I pushed my hands over my ears, but still, the volume grew, and the intensity of the sound was so overwhelming I had to force myself awake, clawing my own skin. My eyes shot open, and I stared into the ceiling, heart still pounding, my nails still dug into my thigh. While images of Julie's dangling head flickered before my eyes, I kept repeating the same sentence over and over again.

"I am not going to let them break your neck. I am not going to let them break your neck. I am NOT!"

CHAPTER SIXTY-NINE

May 2018

I didn't sleep any more that night. The nightmare lingered with me so deeply the next morning, I couldn't eat. I drank some coffee instead, and headed out the door, telling Sune I promised I would be back before he left for his training. Tobias was old enough to watch Will for a few hours, but we preferred that he didn't have to with everything that was going on. I simply didn't like to leave them alone.

I wasn't going to stay home all day waiting for a phone call or a text telling me where to find my decapitated daughter. I knew I had to act now to get ahead of these kidnappers.

I drove to the hospital and ran inside where I found Sue and Emmett, sipping hospital coffee. I approached them, and Sue's face lit up.

"Rebekka!"

"How is she?" I asked and gave her a warm hug.

"She's good. Dehydrated and lost a lot of weight, but she's going to be fine," the doctor says. "The pills didn't do any damage to her kidneys or liver."

I looked at the clock. It was only eight in the morning. "Can I see her?"

Sue looked briefly at her husband then back at me with a gentle nod. "Of course. Let me show you in."

Alicia looked pale and weak as I entered, but her eyes shone with a bright light when she saw me. I hurried to her and grabbed her hand in mine. I could hardly get the words across my lips.

"Tell me about Julie, please? Is she still alive?"

Alicia nodded. "She was when I was taken out. She gave me a hug."

I exhaled in relief. "How was she? Was she okay?"

Alicia nodded. "She seemed good. Some of the other girls were sick, but not Julie."

"She told us they were being kept underground."

The voice belonged to Jack. I turned around and saw him enter with a light wave and a cup of coffee in the other hand.

He handed me the cup. I took it, giving him a puzzled glare.

"You look like you need it more than me," he said. "I just got this one from the machine. I'll just get another one later."

"Thank you," I said and sipped the hot cup.

"How are you holding up?" he asked.

I shrugged. "Feel like a plastic bag in the wind, I guess. Constantly being tossed around, completely out of control of what happens to me."

He nodded with an exhale.

"You're saying they kept them underground?" I asked nervously. The very thought made me want to cry.

Jack nodded, then signaled for me to walk with him out into the hallway to give Alicia some peace and rest. I sent her a smile, then followed him.

"She didn't see much, I'm afraid," he said.

I sighed, feeling myself tense up. How was it possible to keep ten children hidden underground?

"They were taken there in a closed van with no windows, and it was dark, both when they got there and when they pulled her out again. All she knows is that it was underground; they walked down into a hole and used a ladder. She tells me she thinks it was a buried truck. A box truck. It looked like the inside of her aunt's moving truck, she told us."

"So, they buried a truck underground, huh?"

"Yes. Stocked it with crackers and cereal that they lived off. Water bottles too and they had even mattresses and boxes they used as toilets. It was all very well planned."

"So, we have no way of finding out exactly where this truck is?"

"I'm afraid not," he said.

"And the kidnappers?"

"She says she can recognize them. They wore stockings, but she says she might recognize their eyes. "

"So, I guess we messed up their plans, huh? They hadn't planned on us finding her alive. Good. I intend to keep that up. I'm done playing their little games."

"Don't do anything silly, will you, please?"

"Of course not. I never do," I said sarcastically. Jack gave me a look. I ignored him.

"Did she mention Mr. Meckler?" I then asked. "When you asked her about the buses and who told her to get on the different bus."

"That's the odd part."

"Why?"

"She said it was a woman's voice. She never saw her face, because there was so much chaos, and she didn't turn around. All she felt was someone tapping her on the shoulder, and then a woman told her to go on the other bus today."

"A woman? Is she sure about that?"

"She says she is."

"So...it must have been Mrs. Baker, then?" I asked.

Jack nodded. "I sent my men out to find her this morning, but she wasn't at her house. We're searching for her."

I stared at him, remembering talking to Mrs. Baker at Juice N' Java a few days ago.

"Really?" I said. "Mrs. Baker? I find that very hard to believe. She's such a sweet old lady?"

"She might not have been the one planning the entire thing; maybe she was just a part of it."

"But why? Why would a sweet old lady like her do such a terrible thing? I don't understand it," I said.

Jack sighed and looked at his phone that was vibrating. "Well, hopefully, we'll be able to get her in, so she can explain all that to us. If you'll excuse me. I have to take this."

"Of course."

"See you later, okay? And remember, don't do anything stupid," he said and rushed off, holding the phone to his ear.

I watched him walk away while praying that it was someone calling to let him know they had found Mrs. Baker.

CHAPTER SEVENTY

May 2018

Julie hugged Nikki extra close. Their underground tomb suddenly seemed so empty and lonely now that all the other girls were gone. Julie hadn't slept at all since she heard the hatch slam shut. She was so scared.

After they had closed the hatch, she had heard them talking outside.

"They're gone," she heard one of them say. She recognized his voice as the same one that had peeked inside and closed the hatch in front of her.

"What do you mean how did that happen? How am I supposed to know?" he then said.

"She's gonna kill us," another voice said. "She's gonna kill us all for letting this happen."

"Calm down."

"How am I supposed to calm down? All we had to do was to make sure those girls stayed down there. It was our only job."

"Damn kids," the first one said. "They can't have made it far."

"I ain't going into those swamps in this darkness," the second one said. "All kinds of animals lurk in there. Snakes, gators, spiders."

"Afraid of a little spider, are we?"

"I ain't doing it."

"All right, all right. Those kids won't survive a night in there anyway."

"So, what do you suggest we do now then? The kids down there have seen our faces."

There was a pause. It sounded to Julie like they were inhaling, and she wondered if they were smoking cigarettes.

"I might have an idea," one of them said. "We don't have to run it by her first."

After that, everything had gone quiet for a few minutes until Julie heard the sound of dirt hitting the hatch once again. She knew the sound so well by now, but now that she knew what it actually was, it felt more claustrophobic than ever. Back when she hadn't known that they filled dirt on top of the hatch, she still believed there was a way out, but now that she knew how long it had taken them to dig through it the last time, the feeling of suffocation was even heavier than before.

She looked down at Nikki, who had absolutely no color in her cheeks anymore. She was so still it was eerie. Her breathing came in ragged sniffs that didn't seem to last long enough to get proper air into her lungs. Julie felt a tear escape her eye and followed it as it fell on Nikki's lifeless face. She wondered what exactly it was the kidnappers had talked about doing, what was going to be their next move? Would it be to kill both her and Nikki? Because they had seen their faces?

Julie sighed and stroked Nikki gently across her burning face, wondering how long a body could sustain having a fever before it caved in. She had to be severely dehydrated by now since she barely had anything to drink, and the little Julie managed to actually get into her mouth probably never even made it inside of her small body.

Julie hugged Nikki and held her tight, rocking back and forth like she used to do to her favorite teddy bear, crying.

We're never getting out of here, are we? This is it, isn't it? Next time that hatch opens, it'll be them, ready to kill us.

CHAPTER SEVENTY-ONE

May 2018

I made it back before Sune had to go. Well, almost that is. I was a few minutes late, and he was a little annoyed with me. I leaned over to kiss him, but he was in too much of a rush to make it to his appointment on time, so he brushed me off instead.

I sat in the living room with my iPad and a coffee but couldn't really sit still. The more we approached the time of day when we usually heard from the kidnappers, the harder it became to remain calm. Was it going to be my turn this time?

I kept checking the phone again and again, and every ten minutes, I would rush to the mailbox to see if they had left a note for me like they did for Alondra's parents.

But nothing happened. The clock approached noon and still nothing. As I watched the minutes go by, I felt more and more anxious. Had someone else received a note from them? Had Jack started the search for someone else? I didn't know if the thought made me feel relieved or even more anxious.

I played a game of Go Fish with Will but couldn't really focus on it, and he kept winning, while all I did was drum my nails on the breakfast counter.

Tobias walked across the room toward the Xbox.

"Hi there, stranger," I said, trying to sound cheerful. "I haven't seen you all morning. Are you all right?"

He nodded without looking at me. "How's Alicia?" he then asked.

"She's going to be fine," I said.

"That's good news, right?"

"It sure is," I said.

"So, now they can get them, right? I mean, she can tell where they were, right? And who the kidnappers were?"

I patted the seat next to me, and Tobias came over to sit.

"I'm afraid it's not that easy, buddy. She did help a little bit, though. She told them it was Mrs. Baker who told her to get on the other bus on the day they disappeared. Now they're all looking for Mrs. Baker, and hopefully, that will lead us to Julie."

Tobias looked pensive. His eyes then rested on me. "Mrs. Baker? But…"

"But what?"

"She…she couldn't have…"

"Why not?" I asked.

"Because she was busy separating Billy and Timmy. There was a fight while we waited. Billy and Timmy as usual. Everyone was watching them, and Mrs. Baker tried to separate them."

"So, everyone was looking at them and not at the woman tapping the girls on the shoulders?" I asked. "Where was Mr. Meckler while Mrs. Baker was taking care of the fight?"

"He went to the kindergarteners to open the doors for them. They always come out last. That's why Mrs. Baker was all alone with Timmy and Billy and separating them."

"So, you're telling me everyone's attention was on the fight, huh?"

I grabbed my phone with the intention of calling Jack when it vibrated in my hand. It was him.

"Jack?"

"They have made a demand. Ten million dollars."

I sunk back in my seat. "You're kidding me, right?"

"Nope. We just received the phone call. Ten million dollars by this time tomorrow."

"But...but why now?"

"My guess is they have become desperate. We weren't supposed to find Alicia alive, and now that we did, they sense we're getting close. They're scared."

"Good," I said. "Now, listen to this. Tobias told me there was a fight when they were waiting for the buses."

"I know that, why?"

"Because he said all eyes were on the fight. And Mrs. Baker was separating the kids."

"Yes, she told us that when we talked to her, but Mr. Meckler couldn't confirm it. What's your point?"

"I think someone else snuck out there and tapped the kids on the shoulders. She could do it completely unnoticed because all of the attention was on the fight."

"A third person, huh? But who?"

"It has to be someone from the school. No one else is allowed on the school grounds. They're very strict about that. Not even parents. They have to wait outside."

"So, what you're saying is it could have been another teacher?"

"Maybe," I said, while someone addressed Jack on the other end and he told me he had to go. We hung up.

I put the phone down, then glanced at Tobias, who poured himself a bowl of cereal when the dime finally dropped.

CHAPTER SEVENTY-TWO

November 2006

"You again?"

Judge Porter looked down at Jane.

"I'm tired of seeing you in my courthouse. We've been at it for almost six years now."

Jane rose to her feet. "I am sorry your honor. I just really want my children back."

Jane sat back down, this time a lot more confident than the past four times she had been in the same family court fighting for her girls. Her lawyer had argued again and again that the children had been removed from her by mistake, but this time they had new evidence. It had come to the lawyer's attention, that it was, in fact, the children's grandmother on their father's side who had alerted the authorities back in the day, not because she was concerned with their well-being but because she didn't want her son to lose her grandchildren. And Jane's lawyer, Scott, had dug into the relationship between the caseworker Colleen West and the same grandmother and found a very suspicious connection that he now argued in front of the judge.

"Colleen West's father suffers from MS and has no insurance to cover the costs of his many hospitalizations and his medications, or at least, so it was until Mrs. Riley, the children's grandmother made sure to change that. See, her other son, the children's uncle and current foster father, Jim Riley, is an insurance agent at a very well-established insurance company and, if you look closely at these contracts here, marked as exhibit 3A and 3B, then you'll see he was the agent who got Mrs. Colleen West's father a very good insurance deal, one that would cost him…well, what do you know? Nothing. And if you look at the date the deal was signed, then what do you see now? It was made only two days after Jane Wilson left her abusive husband in June 1999. A coincidence? Well, you're the judge."

Jane's lawyer sat down, and she felt a shiver run through her body. They had a very strong case, and they both knew it. Never before in the many other times she had sat there in this courtroom had she felt so sure that this time she would win. Heck, this time she more than sensed it, she actually dared to hope that the judge would rule in her favor.

She hadn't seen her girls in almost two years now. And every time she tried to call DCF or even go through the courts, she was told she had no rights, that the children no longer needed her.

She had Matthew with her in the courtroom, sitting in the back with her mother. He was now seven years old and growing up to be such a handsome boy. And sweet too. He was such a joy. But Jane wanted all her family back, all her children. It was her right. They were hers, and she wasn't giving up. The twins were fourteen by now, and she only had a few years left with them before they left for whatever life was destined for them, but if she could only get those four years. If only. Anna and Vanessa were still young, and she could have many good years with them and Matthew. There was still time, she thought to herself, as Judge Porter looked down at her once again, then banged his hammer.

"Court rules in favor of Jane Wilson." Then he scoffed. "You happy? You got your children back. Now, get out of my courtroom. I hope never to have to see your face again."

CHAPTER SEVENTY-THREE

May 2018

Cereal boxes. Flippin' cereal boxes! Why hadn't I thought of it before? I slammed my hand into the wheel of the car a couple of times in frustration. I kept calling Jack Ryder while driving over the bridges, but only reached his voicemail. This time, I left a message.

"Jack, it's me. Rebekka. I'm going back to the quarry. I know where Julie is, and I'm getting her back. Please, come as soon as you hear this."

"Cereal boxes," I mumbled while reaching the mainland. "You should have known, you idiot. Why else would there be cereal boxes in a place like that? Jack even told you; he even said the words, *They stacked the place with cereal boxes.* You were there, Rebekka. You were right there!"

The thought made me want to throw up. To think I could have found the girls earlier and avoided everything that had happened. I could have saved them. I was there! Dang it, I was right there!

I drove for about twenty minutes while the landscape became more and more swampy and desolate, till I reached the quarry. I parked a little away from the entrance, then grabbed Tobias's baseball bat that I had brought with me as the only weapon I could find.

I knew it wouldn't be much against kidnappers who probably had guns, but it was all I had at hand. And, to be honest, I was so angry by now I didn't care if they came at me with cannons or tanks. I was ready to fight to get my daughter back. The way I saw it, there was nothing stronger in this world than a mother fighting for her child.

I ran the rest of the way, whirling dust up around me, then stopped as I spotted the small shack. I snuck up to it, then looked down at my baseball bat. Knowing that the best defense was an attack, I decided a surprise attack had to be better than anything else. With the bat swung over my shoulder I kicked in the door, then rushed inside, swinging it uncontrollably. Inside sat two men, staring at me. One of them pulled out his gun, but I was faster. I swung the bat at him and hit him on the nose. His nose made a strange, eerie crunching sound, and the man screamed, bending forward holding it, dropping the gun to the floor with a loud thud. Seeing this, the other man rose to his feet, pulled his gun at me as well and, as I swung the bat at him, he fired. I screamed while the bullet whistled past me and hit the wall behind me. Before the man could fire again, I swung the bat once more and hit him straight on the ear. The man screamed, and his gun fell to the ground. I picked up both of them.

Panting, I stared at the two men. I had both of their guns pointed at them, both of them shaking heavily in my hands.

"Now...you two...grab those shovels over there and help me dig out the girls."

The two men looked at me like I had lost it. Each of them was bleeding heavily from where I had hit them. One of their noses sat crooked on his face while blood gushed out of his nostrils.

I waved the gun at them to make them understand that I was being serious.

"Don't make me come over there. I'm counting to three, and then you better be grabbing those shovels. Now, MARCH!"

CHAPTER SEVENTY-FOUR

May 2018

I t was so hot that sweat was gushing from my forehead, even though I wasn't the one doing the digging.

The one with the broken nose sniffled and stopped to wipe his forehead.

"No breaks; keep going," I hissed.

The man continued. Dirt flew in the air, and soon I could see a hatch. I felt my heart begin to race inside my chest. At the same time, I wanted to cry. To think that they had kept the girls, my daughter, underground like that for all this time. It made me want to kill them right there on the spot. The anger toward them felt unbearable.

The man with the bleeding ear stopped digging. I approached the hatch. "Down there?" I asked, then swallowed the lump in my throat. "You pigs kept them down there?"

"They ain't down there," the one with the bleeding nose said.

I stared at him. My hands were getting sweaty and slippery. "What do you mean they're not down there?"

"They ain't down there no more," he repeated.

"I don't believe you," I said.

"They did, they ra…" the guy stopped when he received a look from his friend with the bleeding ear.

"You won't find them till we get our money," the ear-guy said. He exchanged a glance with the other guy, and I sensed something was off.

"You're lying," I said and lifted the guns up to let them know I wasn't letting my guard down. "Open the hatch."

The one with the bad ear leaned forward and grabbed the hatch, then pulled it open.

"See for yourself."

As he said the words, the one with the bleeding nose moved so fast I didn't react fast enough to fire the guns. He grabbed me and lifted me in the air, then threw me inside the hole and closed the hatch as I fell into the darkness. I screamed, but luckily, I landed on a bunch of mattresses. Both guns fell in with me and landed on the floor beneath me.

It took a few seconds for my eyes to get used to the darkness, but as they did, I managed to look around. The worst part was the stench. It made my eyes water, and the stuffiness of the place made it so hard to breathe that I gasped for air.

I climbed down the mattresses, desperately looking to see if I could spot Julie anywhere, but the place seemed empty. Except for something in the corner, a small bundle that was all curled up. As I approached it, I realized it was a little girl. I used my phone to shine a light on her, then walked closer till I could see her face.

"Oh, my God, Nikki," I exclaimed and turned her around. She was barely alive. I fumbled with my phone to call for help, but there was no signal. Panic spread quickly through my body.

Find a way out of this place. Fast. You need to get her out of this place now. She needs to go to a hospital!

As I allowed the panic to settle in my body, there was a sound coming from above me and, seconds later, the hatch opened once again and let in the wonderful sight of the sun's light. Thinking it was the kidnappers again, I grabbed for one of the guns and pointed it up, finger on the trigger, ready to shoot as soon as I spotted a face.

CHAPTER SEVENTY-FIVE

May 2018

S econds later, a face appeared, but I couldn't see it properly. I moved my finger on the trigger when a bright light shone in my face, and a well-known voice filled the air.

"Don't shoot, Rebekka, it's me!"

My finger slipped on the trigger, much to his luck, and I lowered it before I could hurt him.

"Jack?"

I walked closer and saw his face properly.

"Didn't I tell you to stay out of trouble, huh? How's that going for ya'? Lucky for you, we arrived just in time to see them throw you in there."

"Call for an ambulance," I said. "I have one of the girls down here, and she needs medical attention as quickly as possible."

"Call for an ambulance," Jack yelled to whoever else was up there with him, then looked back down at me. "Let's get you out of here. My men found a ladder by the old shack. We're bringing it down."

I grabbed Nikki in my arms and, seconds later, I was climbing up toward the fresh air with her in my embrace. I couldn't believe how light she was. As I approached the opening, Jack reached down, grabbed Nikki, and pulled her out first. I kept crawling till I reached the end, then took one last glance down at what had been my daughter's prison. It felt almost like the many empty cereal boxes were mocking me. I wondered for a second if I would be able to keep myself from killing the person who had exposed my daughter to this once we had her. I wasn't sure.

I turned toward the light, then climbed up. I was helped up the last part by Jack's strong arms. As I once again set foot on the ground, I took in a deep breath of fresh air and exhaled. In the distance, I could see the two men I had mutilated with my bat being taken away in police cars.

"She's not there, Jack. She wasn't there. None of them were. Except for Nikki," I said. "I think they left her because they thought she would be dead soon anyway, or maybe they thought she already was dead."

Sirens wailed as the police cars left with the two men and, in the distance, I spotted the ambulance approaching.

"Where are they, Jack? Where's Julie?"

"They must have moved them. Probably knowing that we were onto them after Alicia was rescued. At least we got two of them."

"You saw Nikki's condition," I said. "None of them can be doing well. We need to get to them."

"I know," he said. "I know. But we are getting closer. I know that several of the parents are looking into getting the money together."

I felt something go through me as he said the words. I turned to look toward a row of tall trees in the background where the swamps began.

"The mattresses," I said. "They were stacked."

"So?"

I looked at Jack. "They ran away. The guy with the bleeding nose almost told me so, but his friend stopped him. Because he knew that they would never get their money if I knew the girls had run away. They must have stacked the mattresses to get to the hatch, then dug their way out. They were bluffing, Jack. They're bluffing us."

CHAPTER SEVENTY-SIX

May 2018

Jack sent all his men into the swamps. The local police force arrived with airboats, and Jack called in helicopters to circle the entire area.

The first girl they brought out was Tonya. She was completely out of it, sunburned and dehydrated, but she was alive.

Next came Trudy and Britney, who told us they had stuck together through the night and slept in a tree. Aubrey was passed out and had been bitten by a snake, but luckily not a venomous one. It took hours, but by the time the sun was about to set, they brought out Hayley, completely undernourished and dehydrated, but alive. I ran to her as they put a blanket around her shoulders.

"Haley. Have you seen Julie? Where is she?"

Haley stopped and looked up at me. I had never seen such deep exhaustion in a child before.

"She didn't want to leave Nikki…"

I swallowed hard. "Nikki? But she…she was still…"

Haley shrugged, and the officers guided her toward an ambulance waiting to bring her to the hospital. I looked after her as she was escorted away, my heart pounding in my chest.

They had all made it out? But Julie had gone back? For Nikki?

But Nikki was still down there? She was still in the hole underground.

I turned to face Jack, tears springing to my eyes. He pulled me into a warm embrace and held me so tight I could hear his heartbeat.

"Where is she, Jack? Where's my little girl?" I sobbed.

"We'll find her. We'll find her. I'll make sure we do."

I closed my eyes and tried hard to let his words convince me he was right, but somehow, my hope was dwindling anyway. It was while standing there in his strong arms that I thought about something.

"Nikki is the last one."

I pulled out of his embrace.

"What's that?"

"In the song. You know how it ends with ...*and then there was none.*"

He gave me a confused look. "Yes, and?"

"Well, all the other kids escaped, and only Julie and Nikki were left. That's what we know so far. So, if Nikki was the last one, then Julie..."

"Must be the second to last."

I grabbed my phone and found the lyrics to the song again. I sniffled as I read them out loud to Jack.

"Two little Injuns foolin' with a gun,
One shot t'other
And then there was one."

I stared at Jack and down at the phone's display again. Then I dialed a number. It took me only one phone call to get my suspicion confirmed, a suspicion I had had since I had spoken to Tobias earlier. After that, it took me just a few seconds on my phone to find the place I was searching for.

"Will you drive, or shall I?" I asked Jack. "And don't even try to tell me to stay here while you take care of it because you know I can't do that."

CHAPTER SEVENTY-SEVEN

May 2018

Julie could see nothing but deep darkness. She knew she wasn't in the tomb anymore since they had come down to get her and taken her out. She had screamed and kicked at them, fighting their attempt at taking her out with them. Not so much because she didn't want to get out; of course, she wanted to, but she didn't want to leave Nikki all alone down there. She knew Nikki would never survive if there was no one to take care of her and make sure she had water poured into her mouth.

"She'll die," she screamed. "She'll die!"

But the kidnappers had placed a bag over Julie's head and carried her up and out. Where to, Julie didn't know. At first, she had walked for a little while, still crying and screaming. Then they had placed her inside a van or something like that and had driven for quite a while. Julie had been screaming and yelling in the back, but after a while, she had given up mostly out of exhaustion and laid down and, even though she had fought it, sleep had overpowered her.

When she woke up, she was no longer moving but was lying on what felt like solid ground. She was still wearing the bag over her head, and her feet were tied together. She tried to pull off the bag, but it was tied in the back, and no matter how much she tried, she couldn't get it off. She then tried to loosen her feet, but they were tied with a strip like the ones the police used in movies and, no matter how much she pulled it, she couldn't get it off either. She managed to get onto her knees, and by using the wall behind her, she managed to stand on her feet. She couldn't see anything and tried to run around, but almost fell as she tried to move her feet.

"Hello?"

The sound of her voice bounced off the wall behind her. She thought she could hear a bird in the distance and the sound of cicadas. The air was fresh, so she had to be outside somewhere. But where was she?

"Hello? Is there anyone here? Hello?"

A loud sound coming from not too far away made the blood in her veins freeze over. Even though Julie had never actually seen a gun in real life, she had no doubt in her mind that she had just heard one being cocked.

CHAPTER SEVENTY-EIGHT
May 2018

Matt's shooting range was located on Merritt Island, the island between Cocoa Beach and the mainland. Jack parked in the parking lot outside, and we rushed out.

"Are you sure about this?" he asked on our way in.

"I'm positive. The place belongs to her son. Matthew Riley is her son. Judge Emmett Porter explained it all to me when I called him earlier. Matthew is her son. I searched it and found out that he recently bought this place with the money he inherited from his father when he was killed in a fire two years ago. I'll give you the details later. Trust me on this. "

He sighed. "Whatever you say."

"It fits with the song too," I said and grabbed the door. I opened it, and we hurried inside. More police cars arrived, and officers jumped out, then surrounded the area. I didn't care if I was caught in between anything. I just wanted my daughter back. I found the sign pointing to the shooting range, then ran. Jack had already pulled his gun and pointed it at anyone trying to get in our way.

"Out here," I said and pointed. In the distance, I spotted the shooting range, and it didn't take me very long to see my daughter. She was standing in front of a wall, the black target figure behind her, a bag over her head, feet tied together. Inside the booth, ready to shoot, I spotted a person, her gun pointed at my daughter.

"Stop," she said as we approached her. "Or I'll shoot her."

"Elaine," I said. "Please don't do this. Please, Elaine."

"Actually, it's Jane," she said. "Elaine is my middle name, but you already know that, don't you?"

"Jane, please."

"It's a bitch, isn't it? Not knowing what will happen to your child. Worst feeling in the God-dang world, am I right? Not knowing where she is, if you'll ever see her again. Not knowing if whoever is with her will take proper care of her. Will she be fed? Will she go to bed with a beating? Will I ever see or hold her again? Feel her soft hair? Makes you feel completely powerless, am I right? That someone can simply take your kids from you just like that. Even when your kids realize mommy can't protect them, it destroys something between you that will never come back."

Julie tried to walk but fell face-first into the dirt. Elaine pointed her gun at her while she tried to get up, her finger lingering on the trigger. My heart was racing so fast I wondered if it would actually jump out of my chest. It was unbearable to be this close to my daughter and not be able to hold her in my arms, not be able to save her.

"Let her go, Elaine," Jack said pointing his gun at her. "It's over."

Elaine laughed, then fired a shot. I screamed as I watched the bullet whistle through the air and hit the human-shaped black target on the wall behind Julie right in the heart. Julie screamed too, then rose to her feet and tried to jump away, but Miss Elaine fired another shot right in front of her, and that made her turned around.

"Well. *Whad'ya know?* It's like one of those games at the fair, hah!" she exclaimed.

"Please, stop shooting, Elaine. Please, don't hurt her," I pleaded. "Why are you even doing this? I mean…I get that you wanted us to feel what you went through when losing your girls. It makes sense, in a deranged sort of way, but why? I spoke to Judge Porter earlier, and I asked him if there was anyone at the school whom he knew from his courtroom, and he told me you were the only one. But he also told me he saw no reason why you would want to hurt him or his family since you had your children back. You got them back."

Miss Elaine turned her head and looked at me for the first time, her hands still clutched around the gun.

"Oh, he said that, did he?"

CHAPTER SEVENTY-NINE

November 2006

J ane couldn't contain her excitement. She had been sitting in the waiting room at the local DCF, waiting for at least an hour. But it didn't matter that she had to wait. She had the letter in her hand, holding onto it tight, never letting go of it again. She had read it over and over again when her lawyer had handed it to her and could hardly believe it. The judge had actually given her children back. They had won. Jane had won.

Tears had streamed down her cheeks the first time she read it, and they had done it again the second and third and even the tenth time she read it out loud to herself at home. And tears were rolling down her cheeks once again now as she waited in the room, sitting in the blue chairs with her lawyer, who kept squeezing her hand telling her *any minute now*.

Jane looked at her nails. She had dressed up in her best dress, the long one with the flowers, the one she had also worn to court on the day Judge Porter had finally decided to give her the girls back. It had become her lucky dress and, even though it had become a little tight in the sides because she had gained weight the past few years while longing for her children and eating to find comfort, she still looked very presentable in it. At least, according to her lawyer.

And today, she wanted to look her very best. It was the best day of her life. Finally, she was going to bring her girls home, and they could become a family again.

"What's taking them so long?" her lawyer said and rose to his feet, finally losing his patience.

"It's okay, Scott," Jane said. "We have the letter, remember? They can't deny us the girls. They can't keep them from us anymore, remember?"

Scott nodded, then paced back and forth. Jane didn't share his worry. Not this time. She knew everything would turn out for the best for her. Colleen had been arrested and was being investigated by the police. Jane hoped she would be sent away to prison for a very long time. That seemed like the appropriate punishment for all the torment she had put Jane through over the years. Scott had suggested suing the DCF for years of emotional distress, but Jane didn't want any of that. All she wanted was her girls back, and that was exactly what she was getting now.

"I can't believe it's taking this long," Scott said and looked at his watch. "I have a meeting in half an hour. They better get them here before…"

Barely had he finished the sentence before the door to the waiting room opened. Jane rose to her feet, corrected her dress, then looked at the opening door in great anticipation. She took in a deep breath, then smiled from ear to ear as the caseworker that she had met earlier stepped inside. Behind her, Jane spotted the girls.

Her heart beat so fast, she was about to explode. And then she did. She ran to them, grabbed Vanessa, and held her in her arms, then kissed her and kissed her again and again. She rose to her feet, then grabbed both of the twins and hugged them, holding them so tight they could hardly breathe.

"Oh, my God, girls, oh my…wait. Where's Anna?"

She looked behind the girls, then up at the caseworker, and that was when she noticed that all three girls had swollen red eyes. Elisa was sniffling and looking down at the floor.

Someone stepped up behind the caseworker. Jane's heart literally stopped when she realized it was a police officer. He took off his cap and held it between his hands.

"I'm sorry, ma'am. There was an accident."

CHAPTER EIGHTY

May 2018

"They called it a darn accident. Can you believe it?"

Jane Elaine's eyes glowed with such deep anger, it made her into a completely different person from the nice woman I knew from the front office at the school. I couldn't believe the same sweet lady who greeted me every time I went to the school could also be the vicious woman about to kill my child.

"A freakin' accident!"

"Well, wasn't it?" I asked, glancing at Julie to make sure she was all right. She was on her knees now, crying helplessly. It broke my heart that I wasn't able to simply run in there and get her. Elaine was right about that part. It was the worst feeling in the world not to be able to rescue your child, to fear not getting to her in time.

"Of course not," Elaine spat. "It was no stinkin' accident. He killed her. Her dad did. The girls told me so, but no one believed them. He beat the living daylight out of my poor Anna. I saw her body. So many bruises you could hardly see any skin that wasn't purple or black. Of course, he told them she fell from a tree, and his brother and that stinkin' wife of his chimed in and told them the same story. No one even thought about asking the other children. Because they had a completely different story to tell. But no one would listen. Not the caseworkers, not the police. To them, I was still what it said in their papers, a bad mother whose word you couldn't trust. That was when I swore to get back at them. Get back at all of them. Especially the judge for keeping the kids away from me, but also the entire town for not helping me, for just watching while this was done to my children and me. The school, because they didn't report that my kids were being abused in their foster home. All of you."

I stared at the woman, who still had her gun pointed at my daughter. She sniffled and wiped her nose with the back of her hand.

"They used to love it, ya' know? The song. *Ten Little Injuns.* Especially Anna. I used to sing it to them before bedtime. Anna always asked me to sing it twice. She never could get enough of it."

"Elaine, we have the entire area surrounded," Jack said. "There is no way out for you."

Elaine didn't respond. She kept looking at my daughter, aiming the gun at her.

"What was in it for them?" I asked. "The others?"

"Them? They were nothing but a group of lowlifes Matthew met here at the range when they came here all drunk and crazy and wanting to shoot. We promised them money, thinking we could rip the judge of at least a hundred thousand. But the idiots demanded ten million. Without even asking me. You can put them away for all I care. They mean nothing to me."

"But your son means something to you. And so do your daughters," I said.

She scoffed. "My son is long gone. You won't find him. When you found Alicia alive, I told him to leave. Get away from here. And my daughters? I lost my daughters many years ago. They never really came back to me. They were all so broken after living with their aunt and being beaten by their dad whenever he felt like it. They had been told so many lies about me, there was no saving our family. I know they all blamed me for what happened to Anna; heck, I even do myself some days. I blame myself for not having fought hard enough for them. For not getting to her in time. All three girls left as soon as they turned eighteen and never looked back. Things were never right between us again."

She went quiet while I tried to calm myself down. I had no more pleading left in me. All I wanted was to strangle the woman in front of me, just throw myself at her and hurt her, make her regret she ever hurt my child.

"Ah, she found it," Elaine then said, and lifted her head slightly.

"What did she find?" I asked, surprised.

Elaine laughed. "The gun. I placed a gun out there for her to find."

It took a few seconds before I realized what Elaine's plan was.

"*Two little Injuns foolin' with a gun,*" I said. "It's your way out. You want her to shoot you."

I turned to look at my daughter, fumbling with the gun between her hands.

I opened my mouth to yell at her not to shoot, but it was too late. She had already pulled the trigger. I threw myself to the ground, and Jack did the same. The bullet hit Elaine in the forehead and ripped off a part of her face before she sunk to the ground with a satisfied exhale that almost sounded like she was singing:

"One shot t'other and then there was one."

EPILOGUE

CHAPTER EIGHTY-ONE

June 2018

"**F**ive *little monkeys jumping on the bed.*
One fell off and bumped his head.
Mama called the Doctor and the Doctor said,"

I looked at William and Tobias in the back seat in the rearview mirror when both of them yelled back in unison:

"No more monkeys jumping on the bed!"

Then I laughed. Julie, who was sitting in the front seat, gave me a look.

"Really, Mom?"

"Come on; it's William's favorite song. Sing along, will you? Have a little fun. You're so serious all the time."

Julie rolled her eyes at me as I continued singing. She didn't know it, but it was the most soothing sight to me. Her being annoyed with me was a sign she was back to being her pre-teen self again. I never thought I would have missed it so much, but I had.

After she had shot Miss Elaine at the shooting range, I had yelled at her to drop the gun and to stand completely still; we were coming for her. She had then fallen into my arms, crying helplessly. They took her to the hospital where she got hydrated but, other than that, they said she seemed fine, better than most of the other kids that had escaped. Some of them were on strong antibiotics and fighting bad bacterial infections, due to the exposure to human feces inside the box truck.

Julie had then fallen into a deep sleep, holding my hand, and not woken up until twenty-four hours later, still clutching my hand in hers. By then, a nurse came in and told us Nikki had woken up, and so had Emmy and Aubrey. Later that same day, they had all gathered inside Nikki's room and cried and hugged and talked so much that Julie was completely exhausted afterward.

All nine girls had returned a week later to school—under much media attention—and the small town of Cocoa Beach began licking its wounds and was slowly trying to get back to normal again. At their latest meeting, the city council had decided to name a street after Alondra Browning, in her loving memory.

Julie was struggling with the fact that she had killed someone and was suffering from night terrors and claustrophobia. She was terrified of me leaving her alone. She could suddenly burst into tears for no apparent reason and was sleeping with me most nights, waking up in terrified screams, desperately clinging on to me. I had sent her to see a therapist, and that seemed to be helping her cope with it. She was slowly returning to being herself.

Elaine's son, Matthew Riley, was detained by the police in Canada after a long search, and he had admitted to having watched the children for months before the kidnapping, while they planned their attack. Jack believed they had now captured all who were involved in the kidnapping. Six men in total had been arrested. Including the one who owned the quarry, who had admitted to letting them bury the truck, but insisted that he didn't know what it was used for.

In Miss Elaine's apartment, they had found drawings and notes describing the plan in detail on her computer, and they also suspected her of being behind the fire that killed both her ex-husband and his brother and wife two years earlier.

School was out now for a summer break I think we all needed more than ever. Hopefully, we would be able to put it behind us once we returned in August. I knew I was ready to move on.

. . .

I parked the car in the parking lot outside Dr. Herman's clinic, then looked at the kids. Sune was almost done with his treatment and only had a couple of months left. We hadn't really discussed what would happen then. Would we go back or stay? Sune said he loved it here so much he wanted to stay. Our visas lasted for five years, and we might as well make the best of it, was his argument. I didn't know if I agreed. Had you asked me before the kidnapping, then yes, I would have loved to stay. But right now, I felt like there were so many bad memories in this place. And I was beginning to miss my home in Denmark. There was also the matter of my dad. He wasn't getting any younger or better, and I didn't want to spend his last years so far away from him. So, you could say I was quite unde-cided. It was a conversation we would need to have soon, but not today.

Today was a happy day. I had taken the kids to the clinic to surprise Sune. We wanted to see him train and then take him out for ice cream afterward. To celebrate…well, everything, life. Everything was good right now, so incredibly good.

"Come on," I said and opened the door to the clinic for the kids to swarm inside. William found some toys in the waiting room and played with them while the receptionist told me where to find Sune.

"He's with Kim in room 404."

"All right. Don't tell him we're coming," I said. "It's a surprise."

"My lips are sealed," the receptionist said and mimed that she closed it with a zipper.

"Come on, kids," I said and grabbed William's hand in mine.

We walked down the corridor and found room 404. I could hardly contain my joy as I grabbed the handle. Sune had asked me so many times to come and watch his progress and, finally, I had the energy and time to do so. I couldn't wait.

"Surprise!" I said and swung the door open.

Then I froze.

"Rebekka?"

I closed the door again, barely breathing.

"Dad?" Will said. He looked up at me. I had no words for what we had just witnessed. I felt Julie's hand in mine, while Tobias stood like a rock.

"Why was dad kissing that nurse?" William asked. "And why were they naked?"

The door slammed open behind us and Sune came into the hall-way, still only half dressed.

"Rebekka?"

"Don't even…"

Sune looked at me, flustered. "I'm…I'm…"

"How long, Sune?"

"Rebekka, I…"

"HOW LONG?"

"I don't know…a couple of months?"

I could hardly breathe. "So, while I…while I…and Julie and while everything that was going on…you…and her…How do you live with yourself?"

"Rebekka…please…"

"I can't even look at you right now," I said, and I turned around and grabbed Will by the arm and rushed him and the two others to the car.

"Mo-om?" William cried. "I want to see Daddy. Who was that lady? Who was she, Mommy? Why are we leaving? We can't leave Daddy! How will he get home?"

"Daddy will have to find another way to get home," I said as I started the car up with a roar and backed out of the spot. "He seems to be a lot more resourceful than we have given him credit for. He'll find a way."

THE END

AFTERWORD

Dear Reader,

Thank you for purchasing *Ten Little Girls* (Rebekka Franck #9). It felt great being back with Rebekka and her family again. I hope you enjoyed it too. It's going to be interesting to see what will happen between her and Sune in the coming books.

This was a very scary book to write. You want to know the scariest part? It actually happened. Back in 1976 in California. A busload of children was kidnapped, and the kidnappers hid them in a buried box truck underground in a quarry. Fortunately, the children escaped after sixteen hours by stacking the mattresses. You can read more about it here:

https://en.wikipedia.org/wiki/1976_Chowchilla_kidnapping

Jane's story is unfortunately not only my imagination either. I was inspired by a story of a woman in Denmark who went to a shelter after being beaten by her husband and then had her children taken away from her. Sadly, she isn't the only one. The more I dug into it, there more stories like hers I found. It was scary, and that's when I knew I had to write about it.

Here's the original story that inspired me to write this entire book: https://www.sundayguardianlive.com/culture/single-mother-lost-children-denmark#.WvPCyVYO0Go.facebook

Oh, and about that alligator trick? With the fingers? That actually happened too. A ten-year-old girl was bitten here in Florida and then she jammed two fingers into the animal's nostrils, and it let go of her. See the story here. It's pretty cool.

http://www.nydailynews.com/news/national/girl-survives-gator-attack-sticking-fingers-nose-article-1.3150070

As always, thank you for supporting me, and don't forget to leave a review if you can. It's highly appreciated.

Take care,

Willow

ABOUT THE AUTHOR

Willow Rose is a multi-million-copy best-selling Author and an Amazon ALL-star Author of more than 80 novels.

Several of her books have reached the top 10 of ALL books on Amazon in the US, UK, and Canada. She has sold more than six million books all over the world.

She writes Mystery, Thriller, Paranormal, Romance, Suspense, Horror, Supernatural thrillers, and Fantasy.

Willow's books are fast-paced, nail-biting pageturners with twists you won't see coming. That's why her fans call her The Queen of Plot Twists.

Willow lives on Florida's Space Coast with her husband and two daughters. When she is not writing or reading, you will find her surfing and watching the dolphins play in the waves of the Atlantic Ocean.

Copyright Willow Rose 2018
Published by BUOY MEDIA LLC
All rights reserved.

No part of this book may be reproduced, scanned, or distributed in
any printed or electronic form without permission from the author.
This is a work of fiction. Any resemblance of characters to actual
persons, living or dead is purely coincidental. The Author holds
exclusive rights to this work. Unauthorized duplication is prohibited.

Cover design by Juan Villar Padron,
https://www.juanjpadron.com

Special thanks to my editor Janell Parque
http://janellparque.blogspot.com/

**To be the first to hear about new releases and bargains—
from Willow Rose—sign up below to be on the VIP List.** (I
promise not to share your email with anyone else, and I won't clutter
your inbox.)

- Sign up to be on the VIP LIST here :

http://bit.ly/VIP-subscribe

Tired of too many emails? Text the word: "willowrose" to
31996 to sign up to Willow's VIP text List to get a text alert with
news about New Releases, Giveaways, Bargains and Free books
from Willow.

Follow Willow Rose on BookBub:
https://www.bookbub.com/authors/willow-rose

Connect with Willow online:

- https://www.facebook.com/willowredrose
- www.willow-rose.net
- http://www.goodreads.com/author/show/ 4804769.Willow_Rose
- https://twitter.com/madamwillowrose
- madamewillowrose@gmail.com

Lightning Source UK Ltd.
Milton Keynes UK
UKHW010207070223
416581UK00020B/734/J

9 781954 139657